PENGUIN CLASSICS

A HERO OF OUR TIME

MIKHAIL YURIEVICH LERMONTOV was born in 1814. After his mother's death in 1817 he was brought up on his aristocratic grandmother's estate and separated from his father. Educated at home, he twice made journeys to the Caucasus and then studied in the Moscow Noblemen's Pension and the University (1830–32), although without sitting examinations. He then entered St Petersburg Guards' School and began writing poetry and autobiographical dramas in prose. In 1834 he was made an officer in the Guards Hussars. On Pushkin's death in 1837, Lermontov was arrested for a poem of invective against court circles, *The Death of a Poet*, and was consequently expelled from the Guards and sent to the army in the Caucasus. When he returned to the capital he became involved in a duel and was banished again to the Caucasus in 1840. He was twice cited for bravery, but the Tsar refused to give him the award. On leave in 1841, hoping to retire and devote himself to literature, he was ordered back to the forces. He was challenged to a duel by an officer, over some trivial insult, and was killed on the spot. Lermontov is renowned as the one true Romantic poet produced by Russia and the one who reflected most strongly the current trend of Byronism. Many of his poems were set to music – *Borodino* and *The Cossack Lullaby* became popular songs and *The Demon* was made into an opera by A. Rubenstein. His other poems include *The Novice*, *The Prayer*, *Novgorod*, *The Prophet* and *My Country*. Lermontov greatly influenced Dostoyevsky and Blok; while Tolstoy and Chekhov regarded his prose as a model.

PAUL FOOTE was born in Dorset in 1926. He was, until his retirement, a University Lecturer in Russian and Fellow of The Queen's College, Oxford. His publications include translations of Tolstoy's *Master and Man and Other Stories* (Penguin Classics) and Saltykov-Shchedrin's *The History of a Town* and *The Golovlevs*.

MIKHAIL LERMONTOV

A HERO OF OUR TIME

REVISED EDITION

Translated with an Introduction and Notes by
PAUL FOOTE

PENGUIN BOOKS

PENGUIN BOOKS

Published by the Penguin Group
Penguin Books Ltd, 80 Strand, London WC2R 0RL, England
Penguin Putnam Inc., 375 Hudson Street, New York, New York 10014, USA
Penguin Books Australia Ltd, 250 Camberwell Road, Camberwell, Victoria 3124, Australia
Penguin Books Canada Ltd, 10 Alcorn Avenue, Toronto, Ontario, Canada M4V 3B2
Penguin Books India (P) Ltd, 11 Community Centre, Panchsheel Park, New Delhi – 110 017, India
Penguin Books (NZ) Ltd, Cnr Rosedale and Airborne Roads, Albany, Auckland, New Zealand
Penguin Books (South Africa) (Pty) Ltd, 24 Sturdee Avenue, Rosebank 2196, South Africa

Penguin Books Ltd, Registered Offices: 80 Strand, London WC2R 0RL, England

www.penguin.com

First published in Russian 1840
This translation first published 1966; revised edition published 2001

024

Copyright © Paul Foote, 1966. Revised edition © Paul Foote, 2001
All rights reserved

The moral right of the translator has been asserted

Set in 11.5/13 pt Monotype Fournier
Typeset by Rowland Phototypesetting Ltd, Bury St Edmunds, Suffolk
Printed in England by Clays Ltd, St Ives plc

ISBN-13: 978–0–140–44795–8

www.greenpenguin.co.uk

ALWAYS LEARNING   **PEARSON**

CONTENTS

ACKNOWLEDGEMENTS

The present translation has been made from the edition prepared by B. M. Eikhenbaum and E. E. Naidich and published by the Academy of Sciences, Moscow, in 1962. I should like to repeat my thanks to Gwyn Griffith, Ronald Hingley and John Simmons for the help they gave when this translation was first done thirty-five years ago; in preparing the revised edition I have benefited from the helpful comments and advice of Rosemary Giedroyć, Tim Binyon and Roger Pearson, and the support of Kai and Kiri Eason.

CHRONOLOGY

1814 2/3 October Mikhail Yurievich Lermontov born in Moscow, only child of Yurii and Marya (née: Arsenieva) Lermontov. The Lermontovs descended from George Learmonth, a Scot who entered Russian service in the early seventeenth century.

1817 Death of mother. Father, on bad terms with his wife's family, accepts 25,000 roubles from his mother-in-law, Elizaveta Alexeevna Arsenieva, and departs, leaving Lermontov's upbringing to her. Childhood spent mostly on Arsenieva's estate of Tarkhany in Penza province.

1820, 1826 Accompanied his grandmother to the Caucasus on visits to her sister, resident near Kizlyar and in Pyatigorsk (then Goryachevodsk).

1828 Now settled in Moscow, Lermontov enters the Moscow University Pension for the Nobility. Friendship with the Lopukhin family (Varvara, the second daughter, a lasting attachment). First poems – lyrics and narrative poems on exotic themes (*Circassians*, *Prisoner of the Caucasus*, *The Corsair*). Steady output of verse while in Moscow.

1830 Enters Moscow University (Moral-Political Faculty). Writes two Schilleresque dramas, *The Spaniards* (in verse) and *Menschen und Leidenschaften* (in prose; the title – *Men and Passions* – thus, in German). First publication: a poem in the journal *Ateney*.

1831 Death of father.

1832 Leaves the university without completing the course. Enters military school (School for Guards Subalterns and Cavalry Cadets) in St Petersburg.

1834 Commissioned as cornet in the Life Guards Hussars. His military and social life centres on St Petersburg and Tsarskoe Selo (the nearby imperial palace). First attempt at prose-writing: an historical novel, *Vadim*, never completed.

1835 His narrative poem *Hadji-Abrek* published, without his permission, in the August issue of the *Reader's Library*. Completes first version of his play *Masquerade*, which is rejected by the censors. Marriage of Varvara Lopukhina to N. F. Bakhmetev.

1836 In St Petersburg and on leave in Tarkhany. Makes acquaintances in St Petersburg literary circles. *Masquerade*, amended, again rejected by the censors. Begins *Princess Ligovskoy*, a novel with affinities to *A Hero of Our Time* (abandoned after nine chapters in 1838).

1837 February: Lermontov's poem 'Death of a Poet' on Pushkin's death (January) leads to his arrest and transfer to a dragoon regiment serving in the Caucasus. Reaches Stavropol in May; travels extensively in the course of duty ('I travelled the whole length of the Line from Kizlyar to Taman'); spends time in Pyatigorsk, Zheleznovodsk (where he takes the cure), Taman and Tiflis. Spa society includes some literary acquaintances and political exiles. October: grandmother secures his recall; he is transferred to the Life Guards Grodno Hussars, stationed in northern Russia. December: leaves Stavropol for Moscow.

1838 Arrives in St Petersburg, joins his regiment in Novgorod province. Reinstated in the Life Guards Hussars, returns to service in the capital and Tsarskoe Selo. Mixes in society and on the fringe of court circles: he is befriended by Zhukovsky (aged pioneer Romantic poet, courtier and tutor to the Tsarevich) and the widow and family of Karamzin (the leading Russian Sentimental writer and historian of

Russia); his reputation as the champion of Pushkin establishes him in literary circles, his new poems are published in the leading journals. Begins work on *A Hero of Our Time*.

1839 Military, social and literary life in St Petersburg as before. Completes the final redaction of his long poem *The Demon*, begun ten years earlier. As well as many poems, two parts of *A Hero of Our Time* published in the journal *Notes of the Fatherland*: 'Bela' (March) and 'The Fatalist' (November). In December promoted lieutenant (*poruchik*). The French ambassador de Barant placated on requiring assurance that slighting references to the French in 'Death of a Poet' were not to the French in general but only to D'Anthès (Pushkin's opponent).

1840 February: 'Taman' published in *Notes of the Fatherland*. The same month at a ball Lermontov clashes with de Barant's son and is challenged to a duel. They fight (with swords), and Lermontov is slightly wounded. For this affair he is arrested (March) and appears before a court martial (April). He is posted to the Tenginskii Infantry Regiment, serving in the Caucasus. Publication of *A Hero of Our Time* (April). Spends most of May in Moscow (where he attends Gogol's birthday celebrations) and reaches Stavropol in June. Instead of joining his regiment, he is attached to General Galafeev's expedition into Chechnia and Daghestan. June to November: in action against the forces of Shamil; serves with distinction and is twice recommended for bravery awards which are not approved by the Tsar. October: a volume of his collected verse (including the recently finished narrative poem *The Novice*) published. Active service allows little time for new writing. December: is granted two months' leave.

1841 End of January: arrives in Moscow. From early February in St Petersburg and resumes his previous life in the social and literary worlds. Unsuccessful attempt to retire from the army and engage in literature; considers founding a new journal. Ordered back to his regiment in April, Lermontov travels via

Moscow, where he stays for a week, and reaches Stavropol in May. Assigned to General Grabbe's Daghestan expedition, but is delayed in Pyatigorsk because of illness. July: Major N. S. Martynov, an acquaintance since military school, takes offence at Lermontov's jibes and challenges him to a duel. The duel takes place on 15 July and Lermontov is killed. In his last months he writes some of his best lyrics; second edition of *A Hero of Our Time* (with Author's Preface added) published in the summer.

INTRODUCTION

Lermontov was, after Pushkin, the leading Russian poet of his generation. His literary career spanned a mere dozen years – roughly half of his short lifetime. *A Hero of Our Time*, begun in 1838 and published in 1840, is his only completed novel.

The period in which Lermontov wrote – the 1830s – was a transitional stage in Russian literature when verse surrendered its pre-eminence to the story and the novel and the new age of Realism began. This change in literary perspective was a feature already evident in Western European literatures and Russia rapidly followed the trend. Lermontov's course ran parallel to that of Pushkin, his older contemporary: both poets, while continuing to write verse, turned to prose in the later stage of their careers – Pushkin with *The Tales of Belkin, The Queen of Spades, The Captain's Daughter* and other works; Lermontov, after two abandoned novel projects, with *A Hero of Our Time*.

In his verse, particularly his early works, Lermontov reflected more strongly than any other Russian poet the then current, if waning, Romantic trend of Byronism. However, though he was certainly much influenced by Byron, this does not mean that for him Byronic attitudes were something merely assumed. There were sufficient factors in his life to produce a 'natural' Byronic figure. His mother died before he was three and he was effectively orphaned when his father, after his wife's death, abandoned him to the charge of his wealthy and possessive mother-in-law, E. A. Arsenieva. The divided loyalties of his family life and his

comparative isolation under the cosseting regime of his grandmother helped to develop an introspective, brooding nature in the
child. His early lyrics are full of complaints of loneliness, broken
hopes and distrust of the world. Later his sense of alienation and
bitterness was to be increased by unfulfilled love-affairs – he was
particularly affected by the rupture of his long-standing attachment
to Varvara Lopukhina when she married in 1835 N. F. Bakhmetev,
a man several years her senior.

Born in 1814, Lermontov spent his childhood mainly on his
grandmother's estate of Tarkhany in the province of Penza. The
major events of his early years were the two summer excursions
to the Caucasus, in 1820 and 1826, when he accompanied his
grandmother on visits to her sister who was settled there, with an
estate near Kizlyar and a residence in Pyatigorsk. The impressions
gained then, later to be reinforced by his periods of exile in 1837
and 1840–41, were a dominant influence in his work.

Until the age of fourteen Lermontov was educated at home. In
1827 his grandmother settled with him in Moscow, where, from
1828, his education continued: two years at the Moscow University
Pension for the Nobility, then two years at the university itself.
In these years he began writing ('I started scribbling verse in
1828') and in lyrics, narrative poems, and dramas revealed his
talent – as well as the strong influence of Schiller and Byron. In
1832 he gave up his studies at the university and entered the
St Petersburg military academy (his grandmother again switching
residence). Two years later he was commissioned as a cornet in
the Life Guards Hussars. As a young officer in a fashionable
regiment he moved in St Petersburg society (with which he was
well connected through his grandmother) and engaged in the
usual pastimes of the capital, at the same time cultivating a cynical
disdain for the social world which he frequented. Military duties
and social preoccupations left him little time for literature and he
did not write much in the four St Petersburg years from 1832 – a
few lyrics, some barrack-room verses, one or two longer poems,
the fragment of a novel (*Vadim*) and the romantic melodrama

Masquerade. He appears to have taken no part in the intellectual life of the capital and it was only in 1836 that he began to form any serious connections in literary circles.

The four years preceding his death in 1841 were the most eventful in Lermontov's life. At the beginning of 1837 he achieved sudden fame with his poem 'Death of a Poet', written in response to the killing of Pushkin in a duel which some considered to have been deliberately provoked to destroy him. The poem was an outspoken denunciation of Russian society, including the imperial court, and condemned the 'executioners of Freedom, Genius, and Fame', who had scorned Russia's greatest poet and driven him to his death. Its inflammatory tone and wide circulation in manuscript alarmed the authorities: Lermontov was arrested and, as punishment, was posted to a lesser regiment serving in the Caucasus. On his return to St Petersburg in January 1838 he was greeted as a celebrity, the poetic heir of Pushkin and champion of his memory. Reinstated in his old regiment (again through his grandmother's influence), he resumed his social life as before, but he was now a public poet, acknowledged in literary circles as a serious talent, and new poems by him regularly appeared in print. He had matured as a writer, and, though the old themes of alienation and lost illusions still found a place in his poems, his view of life was broader and more down-to-earth. He wrote robust poems celebrating the virtues of Russians in the past ('Borodino', 'The Song of Tsar Ivan Vasilievich, the young *oprichnik*, and the bold merchant Kalashnikov') and satirizing the manners of mundane society in the present ('The Tambov Treasurer's Wife', 'Sashka'), in which he showed a sharp critical awareness of the world outside himself as well as a talent for writing in the lighter mode. Most of his best work was written or completed in the years 1838–41: lyrics, civic poems, the two major long poems *The Novice* and *The Demon* (both with a Caucasian setting) – and *A Hero of Our Time*.

When *A Hero of Our Time* was published in the spring of 1840 Lermontov was again on his way to the Caucasus. He had been involved in a duel (with de Barant, son of the French ambassador) and was given another exile posting. From June until the end of the year he was engaged in expeditions against the native tribesmen in Chechnia and had little time for writing. He was back in St Petersburg at the beginning of 1841 on two months' leave. While there he sought permission to leave the army in order to devote himself to literature, but his request was refused. His leave over, he returned to the Caucasus for the last time in May 1841. Two months later he was dead. An old acquaintance, Major Martynov, offended by Lermontov's jibes, challenged him to a duel. The duel took place near Pyatigorsk on 15 July and Lermontov was killed on the spot. He was twenty-six years old.

Although Lermontov may have begun writing 'Taman' as early as 1837, serious work on *A Hero of Our Time* began in 1838 after his return to St Petersburg from the Caucasus. Since 1836 he had been engaged on a novel entitled *Princess Ligovskoy*, which has close affinities with *A Hero of Our Time*: the hero, also named Grigory Alexandrovich Pechorin, though not fully developed, can readily be seen as the prototype of the later character; he is depicted in two relationships – one personal, involving the Princess (Vera) Ligovskoy of the title, a former love, now married (recalling the situation of Lermontov and Varvara Lopukhina and anticipating the Pechorin–Vera relationship in *A Hero of Our Time*), the other social, in which Pechorin, upper-class and privileged, clashes with a young official of the deprived lower orders. In the summer of 1838 Lermontov abandoned this potentially cumbrous work and, fresh from his recent Caucasian experience, switched his hero from St Petersburg to the Caucasus and wrote the five compact tales which make up *A Hero of Our Time*. Three of these were first published separately in the journal *Notes of the Fatherland*: 'Bela' (subtitled 'From an officer's notes on the Caucasus') in March 1839, 'The Fatalist' in November 1839, 'Taman' in February 1840. The complete novel appeared in April 1840 and the second edition, for which Lermontov added the Author's Preface, in 1841.

A Hero of Our Time is, as the title indicates, an account of the life and character of a man who is typical of his age. In this it continues the tradition of personal studies, initiated in Russia by Pushkin's 'novel in verse' *Eugene Onegin* (1823–30), but with antecedents in Western European literature, in which the contemporary young man with his problems and faults is exposed. The link between Lermontov's novel and Pushkin's work is evident from a number of similarities: in both the setting is contemporary, the action takes place away from the main stream of social life (in Pushkin the provinces, in Lermontov the Caucasus); the main protagonist in his 'mature' mid-twenties comes into conflict with a pretentious junior, whom he kills in a duel, and arouses the affection of a worthy girl, whom he rejects; there is an onomastic association of the two heroes – Pushkin's Onegin, named after the northerly Russian river Onega, is echoed by Lermontov's Pechorin, named after the still more northerly river Pechora; and in each work the problem of the problematic hero is stated but left unresolved.

Onegin and Pechorin are the first in a line of literary heroes characterized in nineteenth-century criticism as 'superfluous men' and found in the novels of Turgenev, Herzen and Goncharov that followed in the 1840s–50s. Their common feature is that they are misfits, men who are aware that they are above the mediocrity of their society and aspire to something better. They fail – the 'something' to which they aspire is too vague to become a practical goal, conditions of the day provide no scope for them to realize their potential, and, as a rule, they are anyway too feeble of will to achieve anything. A necessary qualification for the role of 'superfluous man' is *consciousness* of one's superfluousness – self-obsession and self-questioning are standard features.

Pechorin only partly fits this pattern. He is cast more in the mould of the Byronic hero, the superior individual at odds with the world. He is proud, energetic, strong-willed, self-assured, but, finding that life does not measure up to his expectations, he has become embittered, cynical and bored. At the age of twenty-five (as he is in the diary section of the book), he has experienced all that life has to offer and found nothing to give him more than passing satisfaction or interest. Life has let him down, failed to provide any purpose worthy of his powers. So he turns against life (that is, people) and dissipates his energies in petty adventures of the kind described in the novel, embarking on them without any illusion that he is doing more than making a temporary escape from boredom.

The only solace Pechorin has is his conviction of his own perfect knowledge and mastery of life. He scorns emotions and prides himself on the supremacy of his intellect over his feelings. 'The turmoil of life has left me with a few ideas, but no feelings,' he tells his friend Dr Werner, and he gives practical proof of this by riding roughshod over the feelings of other people. His disregard for others is repeatedly demonstrated in the novel, and his victims are lucky if they get off with a broken heart (Vera, Princess Mary) – the less fortunate (Bela, Grushnitsky) pay for his distractions with their lives.

Pechorin is not just indifferent to the fortunes of other people – he enjoys persecuting them, and though in some cases the havoc he wreaks on people's lives is unplanned, in others he sets out deliberately to destroy his victims. He talks in his journal of his insatiable desire for power, of the pleasure he derives from destroying others' hopes and illusions, and of people as food to nourish his own ego. His own frustrated ambition and resentment against life turn him into a predator. As he remarks during his carefully planned campaign to win Princess Mary: 'There are times when I can understand the Vampire.' It is particularly this active, aggressive instinct that distinguishes Pechorin from the common run of ineffectual heroes in Russian literature and links him more with Byronic types such as the Giaour and the Corsair.

Pechorin's passion for contradicting others has been bred in his own experience. His whole life, he says, has been a succession of attempts to go against heart or reason. Though he claims that this conflict has been resolved in the victory of reason over feeling, and prides himself on his immunity to emotional experience, this is really a piece of self-deception. He may be free from illusions about life, but he is still subject to the power of his emotions. We see the effect, deep though unexpressed, that Bela's death has on him, the stirring of his old love for Vera, the momentary pity he feels (and suppresses) for Princess Mary as he destroys her happiness. We see his vulnerability in the moments of self-pity when he wonders why it is that people hate him, when he feels dismayed at the destructive influence he has on other people's lives and sees himself not as the controlling genius of his actions, but as a mere involuntary instrument of fate. He has, too, some traces of the idealism he possessed in his youth. His sensitive appreciation of nature is partly due to his recognition in it of the ideal purity and beauty which he finds lacking in human society. In 'Princess Mary' he writes of Pyatigorsk: 'The air is pure, as the kiss of a child, the sun is bright, the sky blue – what more does one want? What need have we here of passions, desires, regrets?'

It is in these moments of self-pity and questioning that Pechorin reveals the dichotomy of his nature. He is gifted with intellect and strength of will, he has a poet's soul and, despite himself, a capacity for emotional experience, yet all he can do is to work off his spite on the weak and innocent. 'I've got an unfortunate character,' he tells Maxim Maximych in 'Bela'. 'If I cause unhappiness to others, I'm no less unhappy myself.' We see that this is only too true and that Pechorin is not just a dastardly villain of romance, but a complex figure, a case for analysis and understanding.

Talking to Princess Mary, Pechorin squarely places the blame for his character on the society in which he grew up. He gives a pathetic account of himself as a child, full of noble ideals and impulses, but frustrated and mocked at every turn by the complacent mediocrities around him. The result, he says, was that he turned from goodness, truth and idealism to cynicism, hatred and evil. Though this confession is calculated to move Princess Mary and win her sympathy (he is gratified to see it brings tears to her eyes), it is a plausible enough tale. Pechorin is certainly to an extent a social phenomenon. It is a commonplace of the 'social' reading of the novel that his generation, which grew up in the repressive early years of Nicholas I's reign, had few opportunities for self-fulfilment or breaking the bonds of conformity, and Pechorin can well be seen as its product. The novel's title *A Hero of Our Time* gives clear indication of the link between its hero and the time in which he lived. Belinsky, the influential critic who wrote the first detailed critique of the novel, emphasized that Pechorin-type figures were inevitable in that particular period of Russian history. 'That is how the hero of our time must be,' he wrote. 'He will be characterized either by determined inactivity or else by futile activity' – that is, by either passive conformity to the social norm or petty rebellion against it.

Pechorin is, though, more than a social type limited to a particular society at a particular time. He is also a psychological type, the dual character in conflict with himself, torn between good and evil, between idealism and cynicism, between a full-blooded impulse to live and a negation of all that life has to offer. This kind of character was one of Lermontov's continual preoccupations and occurs repeatedly in his works – major examples are the fallen angel in *The Demon* and Arbenin, the wife-murderer, in his drama *Masquerade*. In part, this is a reflection of the author's own personality. There is no doubt that Lermontov put a great deal of himself and his own experiences into the novel. The disillusion, cynicism and frustrated striving recorded in Pechorin's journal are recurring themes of Lermontov's lyrics. The vivid observations of the Caucasian natural scene, the life of the military and spa society are Lermontov's, shared by Pechorin. There are autobiographical elements too: the real-life military doctor Maier of Pyatigorsk is reincarnated in Werner; Lermontov's affair with Varvara Lopukhina, terminated by her marriage, is recalled in Pechorin's reunion with Vera; Pechorin in 'Taman' stays in a hovel on the cliff-edge clearly the same as that in which Lermontov had lodged in 1837 (and of which he left a drawing). It was not surprising that contemporary readers saw Pechorin as a self-portrait of the author. It was accepted as such by Turgenev, and Belinsky, who at the time of the novel's publication had a long meeting with Lermontov (then under arrest), also declared the likeness: 'It is himself, just as he is!'

It was in response to such claims that Lermontov wrote the Author's Preface, which first appeared in the second edition. In it he accepts that in his novel he has presented a portrait, but *not* of himself: rather, 'it is a portrait of the vices of our whole generation in their ultimate development'. The denial can hardly be accepted without qualification, for there is evidence enough of the affinity between Lermontov and his hero. On the other hand, there are grounds for accepting his disclaimer since it is evident that by the time he wrote the novel he had detached (or was detaching) himself from his former persona and could take a critical view of the Pechorin type. Lermontov's portrayal of his hero is both subjective and objective: he has the vision now to see Pechorin not only as Pechorin sees himself in his confessional diary, but also as he is seen by a down-to-earth observer such as Maxim Maximych. Lermontov's analysis is both understanding and critical. It is also inconclusive: 'the malady has been diagnosed – heaven alone knows how to cure it!' As for the claim that Pechorin exemplifies the vices of 'our whole generation' one has to look beyond the novel itself. The 'whole generation' to which Lermontov refers is not represented by the other characters of the book, who are mainly (the major exception is Maxim Maximych) social stereotypes, with faults certainly, but none which qualify as 'vices'. A clearer picture of the contemporaries Lermontov had in mind is provided by his poem 'Meditation' of 1838, which opens with the line 'Sadly I look upon our generation . . .' and goes on to catalogue its faults: 'burdened by knowledge and doubt it will grow old in inactivity', it is 'indifferent to good and evil', its 'best hopes and noble voice [are] suppressed', 'there is fire in the blood, yet a certain secret coldness in the soul' – these are certainly vices which Pechorin has 'in their ultimate development'.

The structure of *A Hero of Our Time* is not that of a conventional novel. It is not clear that, when he wrote and published the first of the tales, Lermontov had conceived them as constituents of a novel. The publisher's advance announcement of the entire work referred to it as a 'collection of tales'. The parts are bound into a whole by the single hero, but each is complete in itself (though 'Maxim Maximych' depends on a knowledge of 'Bela', the frame story of which it continues). The novel as a whole has no plot, development or dénouement, but this matters little since the author's purpose was not to write a *history*, but to present a *portrait* of a man of his time. The order in which the episodes are narrated does not correspond to the order in which they happened. The first two 'chapters' – Maxim Maximych's story of Bela told to the travelling officer and the latter's further encounter with him in 'Maxim Maximych' – refer to events that occur *after* those recounted in the three extracts from Pechorin's diary. The chronological sequence of the stories is thus: 'Taman', 'Princess Mary', 'Bela'/'The Fatalist', 'Maxim Maximych', with, in each, a change in location and milieu as Pechorin moves from Taman ('Taman') to Pyatigorsk ('Princess Mary') to the fort at Kamenny Brod ('Bela'), from which, before or after the events described in 'Bela', he visits the Cossack village where he encounters Vulich ('The Fatalist'), and finally Vladikavkaz where he is observed by the travelling officer ('Maxim Maximych').

The telling of the tales is shared by three narrators: in 'Bela' there are two – first, the travelling officer who describes his journey from Tiflis and his encounter with Maxim Maximych, then Maxim Maximych who tells him the story of Bela; in 'Maxim Maximych' the travelling officer is sole narrator; the three tales from the diary are told by Pechorin.

The arrangement of the stories and the succession of narrators provide a broadening perspective as the reader is introduced by stages to the complexities of Pechorin's character. He is first described by Maxim Maximych, the simple, good-hearted old soldier, who can relate Pechorin's actions in the story of his abduction of Bela – but finds the man himself baffling. In 'Maxim Maximych' it is the turn of a more sophisticated observer, the travelling officer, to observe the hero, though their brief meeting allows no more than the opportunity to form certain impressions from his appearance and offhand treatment of his old comrade. This second tale, though it provides a fresh angle on Pechorin, does nothing to explain him, but rather adds to the enigma he presents. With the build-up of interest now complete, the reader is taken on to the self-revelation of Pechorin in the extracts from his diary.

The three sections of the diary – 'Taman', 'Princess Mary', 'The Fatalist' – form a kind of triptych, with a main centre panel flanked by two lesser panels. There is symmetry in the thematic arrangement of the stories: 'Princess Mary', the core panel, is a social novel in miniature presenting Pechorin in his relations with members of his own milieu; on either side are short tales in which, successfully or unsuccessfully, he plays the role of man of action in strange situations. In each of the diary episodes the events described are accompanied by Pechorin's reflections on life in general and his own in particular – minimally in 'Taman', extensively in 'Princess Mary' and 'The Fatalist'. In the self-analytical passages of 'Princess Mary' Pechorin reveals his inner self most clearly. The enigma of *what* he is, which baffled Maxim Maximych, is explained. The enigma of *why* he is what he is is considered in 'The Fatalist'.

As the final 'chapter' in the novel, 'The Fatalist' might be expected to provide the key to what has gone before, but this it does not clearly do. In this story, as in 'Taman', Pechorin is an intruder into another's drama – here, that of Vulich, an obsessive gambler who successfully stakes his life in a game of Russian roulette, only to be killed the same day by a drunken Cossack. Pechorin, having staked *his* life on capturing the killer, reflects on the existence of fate and predestination. Fate is mentioned several times in the novel before 'The Fatalist' – once casually by Maxim Maximych in 'Bela' to explain the singularity of Pechorin ('some people are fated to have unusual things happen to them'), but chiefly by Pechorin in his diary, usually when he seeks to exculpate himself for the disruptive role he plays in other people's lives (in 'Taman': 'Why did fate toss me into the peaceful midst of these honest smugglers?', in 'Princess Mary': '. . . fate always seems to have brought me in for the *dénouement* of other people's dramas', 'How many times have I been the axe in the hands of fate?', 'Why didn't I choose to follow the path that fate had opened to me?'). In 'The Fatalist' Pechorin has no need to excuse his own conduct, but is inclined to accept predestination when Vulich (on whose face he claims to see the mark of death) is fortuitously murdered shortly after escaping death through the misfire of a pistol which should have killed him. Despite this evidence, however, Pechorin says he prefers to take life as it comes and act according to his own free will – which implies the negation of fate as the determinant in human affairs. This apparently serious speculation is given an ironic twist in the final lines of the novel, when Maxim Maximych offers a prosaic explanation for the misfired shot (the unreliability of Asian triggers) and, in the same breath, says he supposes that Vulich had died in the way it was ordained in the book of life. 'The Fatalist' provides no conclusion to *A Hero of Our Time*. Just as Pechorin's malady is diagnosed, but no cure is recommended, so the larger question of life and fate is posed, but left unanswered.

By constructing his novel out of a series of tales told by different narrators Lermontov dispensed with the presence of an all-knowing author. The chosen format proved very satisfactory for its purpose. The five tales provide the evidence for assessing the hero's character; analytical commentary is limited to that provided by Pechorin himself in his diary (part of the evidence) and the non-committal Author's Preface. From all this the reader is left to draw his own conclusions. The economy of the narrative limits the information given about Pechorin to what each narrator knows or, in the case of Pechorin himself, chooses to tell – so, except for a few generalized memories stirred in him by mood or events and the uncertainly reliable account of his past he gives to Princess Mary, we know nothing of the events which made him what he is. The lack of such information serves, if anything, to enhance the interest of Pechorin, and the novel is the better for being untrammelled by digressive explanations of his past. No conventional novel of such short compass could plausibly be so action-packed. Lermontov gives us only 'highlights' and spares us the intervening longueurs of development and daily life. The tales themselves are serious, but not cerebral: they are robust tales of action with all the ingredients of an adventure story – danger, daring, violent death (just averted in 'Taman'), suspense and intrigue, and, as such, make gripping reading which can be enjoyed by readers of different levels of sophistication. The structure of the novel is not without imperfections – it may strain credulity that Pechorin, after his display of world-weary *savoir-faire* in 'Princess Mary', should expect to find happiness with Bela, and fourteen instances of eavesdropping in the extracts from Pechorin's diary is certainly a lot, but, given the pace of the narrative, such things will trouble only the more pernickety critic. It was Lermontov's achievement that he successfully combined a psychological novel with a lively and interesting tale of adventure. It is this which most distinguishes it from the common run of studies of individual psychology written in the early years of the nineteenth century (Chateaubriand's *René*, Constant's *Adolphe*, for instance). The hero is not a closet figure, but a man of energy and action, presented in encounters with smugglers, brigands, fellow-soldiers, salon rivals, and women both homely and exotic. Never, it might be said, a dull moment.

The appeal of *A Hero of Our Time* owes much to its setting in the Caucasus. The area had fascinated Lermontov from boyhood and its landscape and people figured prominently in his early lyrics and youthful narrative poems (1828 *Circassians* and *Prisoner of the Caucasus*, 1831 *Aul Bastundzhi*, 1832 *Izmail-Bei*, 1833–4 *Hadji Abrek*). The fervent declaration he made to the Caucasus as a seventeen-year-old (in the dedication to *Aul Bastundzhi*):

From early years my blood is stirred by
Thy burning heat, thy storms' rebellious blast.
Here, in this northern land thou knowest not,
To thee in heart I'm bound, thine always, everywhere . . .

was no exaggeration. Lermontov's first exile posting to the Caucasus in 1837 broadened his experience and renewed his enthusiasm, which found expression in *A Hero of Our Time*. The exotic landscape allows him to present his hero in sharper focus than would have been possible in the bustle of an urban setting (compare *Princess Ligovskoy*, set in St Petersburg), and Pechorin's harmony with nature is an important aspect of his character. The descriptions of the mountain scenery (Pechorin's and the travelling officer's) are a memorable feature of the novel – they may be repetitive (as is mountain scenery), but they convey well the wonder inspired in any traveller from northern Russia who, after a thousand miles of scarcely undulating plain, is confronted by the highest mountain range in Europe. Besides being a writer, Lermontov was also a considerable artist and left a number of fine paintings of the Caucasian landscape, as well as sketches of local life: the word-pictures in *A Hero of Our Time* owe much to his artist's eye.

The economy of structure in this work is paralleled by Lermontov's economy of style. The narrative is direct and swift-moving, nothing is superfluous. His language is controlled and terse – in this he followed Pushkin, who had defined 'precision and brevity' as the essential principles for prose-writing. Turgenev praised the language of *A Hero of Our Time* for its 'succinctness, precision, and simplicity'. He noted some posturing 'in the French manner', but a few romantic clichés should not be held against Lermontov: when he wrote his novel there was, apart from the recent example set by Pushkin, no developed tradition of prose-writing in Russia. Lermontov showed what could be done in fitting style to context – in the narrative of action, the analytical passages of Pechorin's diary, the descriptions of nature, in society conversation and the homely discourse of Maxim Maximych his language is always appropriately pitched. It was a remarkable achievement for an author of twenty-four. As Chekhov remarked, 'Still just a boy, and he wrote *that*!'

There was lively critical response to *A Hero of Our Time* when it was published. Conservative critics attacked it as an immoral book and a slander on Russian society. Some considered Pechorin an alien import from the West. It was in response to such criticism that Belinsky wrote his long review in which he emphasized the sociological significance of the novel (mediocre society, the man of talent its alienated victim). In doing so he established a line of criticism which has been dominant until recent times. It was followed by later nineteenth-century critics in their studies of the 'superfluous man', which varied in their assessment of Pechorin and his place in relation to society and to the rest of his superfluous brethren; it was strongly continued by critics in the Soviet time, some of whom were prepared to promote Pechorin to the status of revolutionary *manqué*. Relatively less attention has been given to Pechorin as an example of human psychology outside the social context. The debate on the social aspects of the novel has tended to distract critics from considering its qualities as a work of literature, but in recent years this imbalance has been largely corrected and there have been valuable studies on form, narrative method, the place of the novel in the Romantic/Realist tradition and so on, and Western scholars have contributed significantly to these broadening critical approaches. Critics apart, *A Hero of Our Time* has been highly rated by generations of readers worldwide, who appreciate its qualities as a serious socio-historico-psychological novel – and as a cracking good yarn.

Paul Foote

The Caucasus: A Historical Note

The events described in *A Hero of Our Time* relate to the time it was written – the 1830s. The Caucasus then was a new area of the Russian Empire, and though Georgia – which lies south of the main Caucasus range – had been annexed to Russia in 1801, the different tribes inhabiting the mountains that separated the territories of established Russian rule were still unsubdued. In the period of the novel native tribesmen were mounting particularly fierce resistance to the Russian intruders under the leadership of the chief Shamil, an Islamic fundamentalist of the day, who fought the Russians until 1863 (it was in an expedition against him that Lermontov took part in 1840). To protect their territory north of the mountains from incursions by the hill tribes – and to provide a base for further expansion southwards – the Russians had established a series of forts and frontier-posts along the so-called 'Line', which stretched the length of the Caucasus from the Black Sea to the Caspian, roughly following the courses of the rivers Kuban (westwards) and Terek (eastwards). The terms 'left flank' and 'right flank' which are used in 'Bela' and 'The Fatalist' refer to this east–west defence line (from the Russian perspective, 'east' = 'left', 'west' = 'right'). Georgia was linked with the settled territory north of the Caucasus range by the famous Georgian Military Highway that runs from Tiflis to Vladikavkaz, and along which the narrator travels with Maxim Maximych in 'Bela'.

FURTHER READING

On Lermontov's life and works in general

Garrard, John G., *Mikhail Lermontov* (Twayne Publishers, Boston, 1982).

Kelly, Laurence, *Lermontov: Tragedy in the Caucasus* (Constable, London, 1977).

Mersereau, John, *Mikhail Lermontov* (Southern Illinois University Press, Carbondale, 1962). Half the book is devoted to *A Hero of Our Time*.

On *A Hero of Our Time*

Barratt, Andrew and Briggs, A. D. P., *A Wicked Irony: The Rhetoric of Lermontov's 'A Hero of Our Time'* (Bristol Classical Press, Bristol, 1989). Points to a consistent irony of presentation through the novel.

Reid, Robert, *Lermontov's 'A Hero of Our Time'* (Bristol Classical Press, Bristol, 1997).

Turner, C. J. G., *Pechorin: an Essay on Lermontov's 'A Hero of Our Time'*, Birmingham Slavonic Monographs, 5 (University of Birmingham, 1978)

These books offer detailed chapter-by-chapter readings of the novel, in which structure and narrative perspective are explored with broad reference to existing critical views. All are concerned with Lermontov's literary method and intentions, and largely avoid the novel's social-historical reference.

MAP

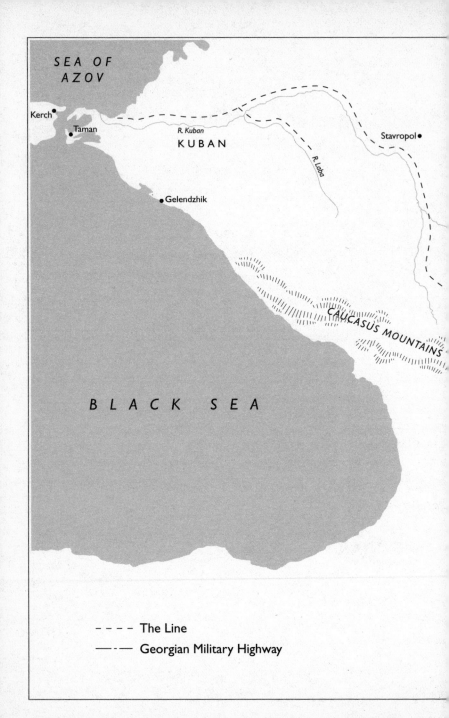

SEA OF
AZOV

Kerch

Taman

R. Kuban

KUBAN

Gelendzhik

R. Laba

Stavropol

CAUCASUS MOUNTAINS

BLACK SEA

- - - - The Line
—·— Georgian Military Highway

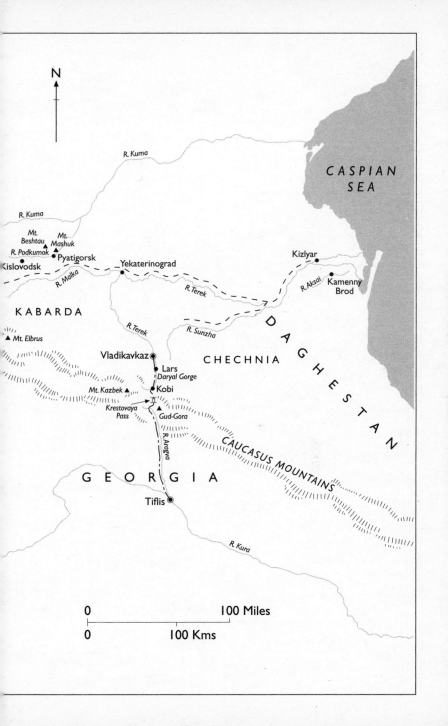

N

CASPIAN
SEA

R. Kuma

R. Kuma

Mt.
Beshtau   Mt.
Mashuk   Kizlyar
R. Podkumok
Kislovodsk   ● Pyatigorsk   Yekaterinograd   Kamenny
                                                                              Brod
                                              R. Terek   R. Aksai

KABARDA   R. Malka

                 R. Terek   R. Sunzha   D A G H E S T A N

▲ Mt. Elbrus   CHECHNIA

                 Vladikavkaz ◉
                              ● Lars
                              Daryal Gorge
Mt. Kazbek ▲   ● Kobi
Krestovaya   ▲
Pass   Gud-Gora

                 R. Aragva   CAUCASUS MOUNTAINS

G E O R G I A

                 Tiflis ◉

                              R. Kura

0   100 Miles

0   100 Kms

A HERO OF OUR TIME

[*Preface*]

The Preface is the first and also the last thing in a book. It either explains the book's purpose or else defends it against the attacks of critics. But the reader doesn't usually care in the least about a book's moral purpose or about journalists' attacks on it, so he doesn't bother to read the Preface. It is a pity, especially in our country, where the reading public is still so naïve and immature that it cannot understand a fable unless the moral is given at the end, fails to see jokes, has no sense of irony, and is simply badly educated. It still doesn't realize that open abuse is impossible in respectable society or in respectable books, and that modern culture has found a far keener weapon than abuse. Though practically invisible, it is none the less deadly, and under the cloak of flattery strikes surely and irresistibly. Our reading public is like some country bumpkin who hears a conversation between two diplomats from opposing courts and goes away convinced that each is betraying his government for the sake of an intimate mutual friendship.

The present book recently had the misfortune to be taken literally by some readers and even by some journals. Some were terribly offended that anyone as immoral as the Hero of Our Time should be held up as an example, while others very subtly remarked that the author had portrayed himself and his acquaintances. Again that feeble old joke! Russia seems to be made in such a way that everything can change, except absurdities like this, and even the most fantastic fairy-tale can hardly escape being criticized for attempted libel.

3

The Hero of Our Time is, my good sirs, indeed a portrait, but not of a single person. It is a portrait of the vices of our whole generation in their ultimate development. You will say that no man can be so bad, and I will ask you why, after accepting all the villains of tragedy and romance, you refuse to believe in Pechorin. You have admired far more terrible and monstrous characters than he is, so why are you so merciless towards him, even as a fictitious character? Perhaps he comes too close to the bone?

You may say that morality will not benefit from this book. I'm sorry, but people have been fed on sweets too long and it has ruined their digestion. Bitter medicines and harsh truths are needed now, though please don't imagine that the present author was ever vain enough to dream of correcting human vices. Heaven preserve him from being so naïve! It simply amused him to draw a picture of contemporary man as he understands him and as he has, to his own and your misfortune, too often found him. Let it suffice that the malady has been diagnosed – heaven alone knows how to cure it!

I

Bela

I was travelling post from Tiflis. The only luggage I had on my cart was one small portmanteau half-filled with travel notes on Georgia. Luckily for you most of them have been lost, but luckily for me the portmanteau and the rest of my things have survived.

The sun was already beginning to hide behind the snowy mountain tops when I entered the valley of Koyshaur.[1] Roaring songs at the top of his voice, the Ossete driver[2] relentlessly urged on his horses so as to reach the top of Koyshaur by nightfall. What a glorious place that valley is! Inaccessible mountains on all sides, red-hued cliffs hung with green ivy and crowned with clumps of plane-trees, yellow precipices streaked with rivulets; high up above lies the golden fringe of the snow, while below the silver thread of the Aragva[3] – joining in embrace with some nameless lesser torrent that roars out of a black, mist-filled gorge – stretches glistening like a scaly snake.

We reached the foot of Koyshaur and halted by the inn. A score of Georgians and hillmen swarmed noisily round the place – a camel caravan had halted near by for the night. I had to hire some bullocks to pull my cart up this confounded mountain, since it was already autumn and there was ice on the roads, and the climb some two miles long.

There was nothing else for it, so I hired six bullocks and a few Ossetes. One of them heaved my portmanteau on to his shoulders and the others helped the bullocks along, doing little more than just shouting.

My own cart was followed by another pulled by two pairs of bullocks as if it was the easiest thing in the world, although it was piled high with luggage. I found this very surprising. The owner of the cart walked behind it, smoking a little Kabarda pipe[4] mounted with silver. He was wearing an officer's frock-coat without epaulettes and a shaggy Circassian fur cap. He looked about fifty. His swarthy complexion betrayed a long acquaintance with the Transcaucasian sun, and his prematurely grey whiskers accorded ill with his firm step and brisk appearance. I went up to him and bowed. He returned my bow in silence and puffed out an enormous cloud of smoke.

'We seem to be going the same way.'

He bowed again without speaking.

'You'll be going to Stavropol,[5] I expect?'

'Yes, sir . . . Carrying government property.'

'Can you kindly tell me how it is that four bullocks can pull your heavy cart with no trouble at all, while six can hardly move my empty one, even with these Ossetes to help?'

He smiled craftily and gave me a knowing look.

'You won't have been long in the Caucasus?'

'About a year,' I answered.

He smiled again.

'Why, what of it?' I asked.

'Oh, nothing. Fearful rogues, these Asiatics are. Do you really think they're doing any good with all that shouting? God alone knows what it's all about! But the bullocks understand them. You hitch up twenty bullocks if you like, but they won't budge an inch when they shout at them in that language of theirs. Dreadful scoundrels they are! But what can you do to them? They like to fleece travellers . . . They've had it too soft, the villains. And just you wait and see – they'll have a tip out of you too. But I know them, they'll not catch me.'

'Have you served here long?'

'Oh, yes, I was here in Alexei Petrovich's time,'[6] he said with some dignity. 'I was a second lieutenant when he came to the

6

Line,'[7] he added, 'and I was promoted twice under him for actions against the hillmen.'

'And now you're . . . ?'

'Now I'm with the Third Line Battalion. And what about you, if I might ask?'

I told him.

Our conversation ended and we walked on side by side in silence. At the top of Koyshaur we found snow. The sun went down, and immediately night followed day, as is usual in the south, but in the reflected light of the snow it was easy for us to make out the road which still climbed uphill, though now less steeply.

I had my portmanteau put back into the cart and the bullocks replaced by the horses. For the last time I looked back down into the valley, but it was completely covered by a thick mist billowing out of the gorges. There was not a sound from below. The Ossetes crowded round me clamouring for a tip, but so sternly did the captain shout at them that they scattered in a moment.

'Ah, these people!' he said. 'They don't know the Russian for "bread", but they've learnt to say "Officer, tip for vodka". Why, I'd rather have a Tatar – at least he doesn't drink.'[8]

It was still almost a mile to the post-station. It was so still all round that you could trace a gnat's flight by the sound of its humming. On our left lay the black depths of the ravine. Beyond it and before us the deep blue peaks of the mountains, creased with folds and covered by layered snow, stood out against the pale horizon, in which the last glimmer of twilight lingered. Stars began to twinkle in the dark sky and it struck me as odd how much higher they seemed than back home in the north. Bare black rocks stuck out on both sides of the road. Here and there bushes peeped through the snow, but not a single dead leaf stirred, and amid this deathly sleep of nature it was cheering to hear the snorting of the tired post-horses and the intermittent jingling of the Russian harness-bells.

'It'll be a lovely day tomorrow,' I said.

The captain made no reply and pointed to a tall mountain which rose up directly before us.

'What's that?' I asked.

'Gud-Gora.'⁹

'Oh yes, what about it?'

'Look at the way it's smoking.'

Gud-Gora was indeed smoking. Light wisps of cloud crept along its sides, and on its summit lay a cloud so black that it seemed a blot on the dark sky.

We could already make out the post-station and the roofs of the huts around it and could see welcoming lights twinkling ahead, when a damp cold wind got up and moaned in the ravine, and it started to drizzle. I had barely got my cape on before we were in the thick of a snow-storm. I glanced at the captain with a look of awe.

'We'll have to spend the night here,' he said with annoyance. 'You'd never get over the mountains in a blizzard like this.'

'Hi!' he called to the driver. 'Had any avalanches on the Krestovaya?'

'No, sir,' answered the Ossete driver. 'But much snow ready to fall.'

There was no guest room at the post-station, so we were put up in a smoky hut. I asked my companion to join me in a glass of tea, for I had my iron teapot with me – my one comfort during my Caucasian travels.

One side of the cottage was built against the cliff, and three wet, slippery steps led to the door. I groped my way in and collided with a cow (the cow-shed takes the place of the servants' hall in these parts). What with bleating sheep and a dog growling, I had no idea which way to go. Luckily I caught sight of a dim light glinting to one side which helped me to find another door-like opening. I was presented with a scene of some interest. The roomy hut, its roof supported on two smoke-blackened posts, was full of people. In the middle of the room burned a crackling fire, laid on the bare earth, and the smoke, driven back through the hole in the roof by the wind, hung so thickly over everything that I was some time getting my bearings. By the fire sat two old women with a host of children and a lean Georgian, all of them in rags. We had no choice but to settle ourselves down by the fire and light our pipes, and before long the teapot was singing merrily.

'They're a pathetic lot,' I said, pointing to our filthy hosts, who were watching us in a sort of dumb stupor.

'As stupid as they come!' he replied. 'Believe it or not, but they're absolutely useless. And you can never teach them anything either. Say what you like about our friends the Kabardians or the Chechens[10] – robbers and vagabonds they may be, but they're plucky devils for all that. Why, this lot don't even bother about weapons. You'll never see one of them wearing a decent dagger. There's your Ossete for you!'

'Have you spent long in Chechnia?'

'I had about ten years there with my company in a fort near Kamenny Brod.[11] Do you know it?'

'I've heard of it.'

'Ah, those cut-throats gave us a time of it! They're quieter now, thank heavens, but once if you went a hundred yards from the stockade there'd be some shaggy devil on the look out, and you'd only to blink an eyelid and before you knew where you were you had a lasso round your neck or a bullet in your head. Grand chaps, though!'

'You must have had lots of adventures?' I said, spurred by curiosity.

'Oh yes, of course. I've had some adventures . . .'

Whereupon he fell to tugging his left whisker, his head bowed in thought. I was most eager to get some kind of yarn out of him – a desire common to all those who keep travel notes. Meanwhile the tea was ready and I took two travelling glasses from my portmanteau, filled one and set it in front of him. He took a sip and said as if to himself: 'Oh yes, I've had some adventures!' This exclamation raised great hopes in me. I know that these old Caucasian veterans like to talk and spin a yarn. They rarely get the chance, since they may often spend four or five years in some god-forsaken place with their company and all that time have no one to say 'Hullo' to them (for the sergeant-major always says 'Wish you good health, sir').[12] And there would be no lack of things to talk about, with strange wild tribes all round them, constant danger and unusual things happening. One can only regret that so little of this is ever put down on paper.

'Have some rum in it?' I asked my companion. 'I've got some white rum from Tiflis. It's turned cold now.'

'Thanks all the same, I don't drink.'

'How is that?'

'I just don't. I took an oath. Once when I was a second lieutenant, you know how it is, we'd had rather a lot to drink, and that night there was an alarm. We went out on parade half-tipsy and didn't half catch it when Alexei Petrovich found out. He was furious. Very nearly had us court-martialled. That's the way of it – you might go a whole year sometimes without seeing a soul, and with vodka on top of that – you're done for.'

At this I almost gave up hope.

'Take these Circassians, for instance,' he went on. 'Once they get drunk on *buza*[13] at a wedding or a funeral, it's sheer murder. I had a narrow escape myself on one occasion, and that was at a friendly chief's.'

'How did it happen?'

'You see,' he began, filling his pipe and taking a draw, 'you see, it was like this. At that time I was with my company in a fort over the Terek.[14] It's getting on for five years ago now. One autumn, when the convoy arrived with the stores, an officer came with it, a young fellow of twenty-five or so. He came to me in full uniform and said he had orders to stay on at the fort. He looked so trim and clean with his uniform all nice and new, I guessed at once that he'd not been long in the Caucasus. "Been posted here from Russia, I expect?" I asked him. "Yes, sir," he said. I took his hand and said: "Glad to see you, very glad indeed. You'll find it a bit dull here, so let's not stand on ceremony. Just call me Maxim Maximych, if you don't mind. And, please, there's no need for full uniform, is there? A field-cap will do when you come to see me." He had his quarters allotted him and settled down in the fort.'

'And what was his name?' I asked.

'His name was . . . Grigory Alexandrovich *Pechorin*. A grand fellow he was, take it from me, only a bit odd. For instance, he'd spend the whole day out hunting in rain or cold. Everyone else would be tired and frozen, but he'd think nothing of it. Yet another time he'd sit in his room and at the least puff of wind reckon he'd caught a chill, or a shutter might bang and he'd shiver and turn pale. Yet I've seen him go for a wild-boar single-handed. Sometimes you wouldn't get a word out of him for hours on end, but another time he would tell you stories that made you double up with laughter . . . Yes, he was a funny chap in many ways. Must have been rich too – from the number of expensive things he had.'

'Did he stay long?' I asked.

'About a year, it was. But how well I remember that year! He led me a dance all right, though I don't hold it against him – after all, some people are fated to have unusual things happen to them.'

'Unusual?' I exclaimed with curiosity, giving him some more tea.

'Let me tell you. There was a friendly chief who lived three or four miles from our fort. He had a son, a lad of about fifteen, who was used to riding over to see us. Every day he came for one thing or another. And it's true, we quite spoilt him, Pechorin and I. And what a daredevil he was – a great hand at shooting or picking up a hat from the ground at full gallop. There was only one thing wrong with him – he had a terrible weakness for money. Pechorin once offered him ten roubles for a joke to steal the best goat from his father's herd. And what do you think? The next night he brought him along by the horns. Sometimes we teased him, and then he'd see red and go for his dagger. "Azamat," I used to say to him, "you'll cop it one of these days. You'll come to a bad end."

'Once the old chief himself came over to invite us to a wedding. He was marrying his eldest daughter and he and I were *kunaks*,[15] so you see I couldn't refuse, even though he was a Tatar. We set off and got to the village with all the dogs letting out a howl to greet us. The women hid when they saw us, and those whose faces we did get a look at weren't much to write home about. "I had a better opinion of Circassian women," Pechorin said to me.

'I grinned. "You wait," I said. I knew what I was talking about.

'The chief's hut was crowded. These Asiatics, you know, are given to inviting all and sundry to their weddings. We were welcomed with due ceremony and shown into the best room. I took care to see where they put our horses though, just in case of anything unforeseen.'

'What happens at their marriage celebrations?' I asked the captain.

'Oh, nothing special. First the mullah reads a piece out of the *Koran*, then the young couple and their relations are given presents. They eat, they drink *buza*. Then there's the trick-riding. There's always some filthy tramp on a miserable broken-down hack ready to show off and play the fool to amuse the company. Then when it gets dark they have what we'd call a ball in the best room with some poor old fellow strumming away on a three-stringed . . . I can't remember the name, anyway it's like our balalaika. The girls and young chaps form up in two lines facing each other and clap their hands and sing. Then one girl and a man come into the middle and sing bits of rhyme at each other, anything that comes into their head, and the others join in the chorus. Pechorin and I were sitting in the place of honour when the host's youngest daughter comes up to him, a girl of fifteen or sixteen, and sings him a – what shall I say? – a sort of compliment.'

'And what was it she sang? Do you remember?'

'Yes, it was something like this, I think: "Our young horsemen are graceful and their coats silver-laced, but the young Russian officer is more graceful than they and he wears braid of gold. He's like a poplar among them, though he'll not grow or blossom in our garden." Pechorin got up and bowed, touching his hand to his forehead and heart, and asked me to reply. I know their language well, so I translated for him.

'When she had gone I whispered to Pechorin: "Well, what do you think of her?"

'"Charming!" he said. "What's her name?"

'"Bela," I said.

'She certainly was good-looking – tall and slim, with black eyes like a mountain goat's that looked right inside you. Pechorin was completely absorbed, his eyes never left her, and she kept stealing glances at him. But somebody else besides Pechorin was taken with the pretty little princess. A pair of blazing eyes were fixed on her from the corner of the room. Looking closer, I saw it was my old friend Kazbich. He was one of those tribesmen you can't be sure about – if they're for you or against you. He'd roused a lot of suspicion, but had never actually been caught at any mischief. He used to bring sheep into the fort and sell them cheap, only he'd never bargain. You had to pay his price, and not for the life of him would he ever come down. They used to say that he liked a trip over the Kuban[16] with the guerrillas, and he looked a proper brigand too – small, wiry, broad-shouldered. And devilish smart he was too, I'll say that for him. His *beshmet*[17] was always tattered and patched, but his weapons were mounted with silver. And his horse was famous through all Kabarda – and right enough too, for you couldn't imagine a finer one. Other horsemen were all green with envy – with good reason – and people tried several times to steal him and failed. I can see that horse now – black as pitch, with legs like steel wires and eyes as fine as Bela's. He was strong too – galloped forty miles at a stretch! And so well trained he followed his master about like a dog and even knew his voice. He never tied him up. The very horse for a brigand he was!

'That evening Kazbich was looking grimmer than ever, and I

saw he was wearing a mail shirt under his *beshmet*. "He's got a reason for putting that on," I thought. "Must be up to something."

'It was stuffy inside the hut so I went out for a breath of air. Night was falling on the mountains and a mist was starting to drift through the valleys.

'I thought I'd look into the shed where our horses were to see if they had fodder. And anyway you can't be too careful – I had a fine horse too and more than one Kabardian had eyed her fondly and said *Yakshi tkhe, chek yakshi*.[18]

'As I was making my way along the fence I suddenly heard voices. One I knew at once – that young scamp Azamat, our host's son. The other one said less and spoke more softly.

' "What are they talking about?" I wondered. "Not my horse, I hope." So I crouched by the fence and listened, trying to catch every word. I was intrigued, but missed some of it because of the singing and talking in the hut.

' "You've got a wonderful horse!" said Azamat. "Why, if I was master here and had three hundred mares I'd give half of them for your steed, Kazbich!"

'So it's Kazbich! I thought, and remembered the mail shirt.

' "Yes," said Kazbich after a short pause. "Yes, you won't find a horse like that in all Kabarda. Once I was on a raid over the Terek with the guerrillas, stealing Russian horses. We ran into trouble and got split up. I had four Cossacks[19] after me. I could hear them shouting, the infidel dogs. There was a thick wood ahead, so I lay flat on the saddle and gave myself into the hands of Allah. For the first time in my life I insulted my horse with a touch of the whip. He went like a bird between the branches. Sharp thorns tore my clothes, dead elm branches hit my face. My horse leaped over tree-stumps and charged its way through bushes. I should have left him as we came into the wood and taken cover among the trees on foot, but I couldn't bear to part with him – and the Prophet repaid me! A few bullets sang over my head and I heard the Cossacks running after me, on foot now. Suddenly before me there was a deep ravine. My horse thought for a moment and jumped. His hind legs came away from the far bank and he was left hanging by his front legs. I let go of the reins and went flying into the ravine. That saved my horse – he sprang clear. The Cossacks saw all this, but no one came down to look for me. They must have thought I'd been killed. I heard them rush to catch my horse. It was agony. I crawled through some thick grass on the edge of the ravine and looked out. The wood ended there, and I saw a few Cossacks riding into the clearing. Then out of the wood comes my Karagyoz[20] and gallops straight at them. They rushed after him shouting and chased him for ages. One Cossack in particular nearly had a lasso round his neck a couple of times – I trembled and looked down and started to pray. A few seconds later I looked up and saw my Karagyoz going like the wind before them, with his tail streaming, and the infidel dogs trailing one after the other over the steppe, their horses quite done in. By Allah, it's true, as true as I stand here! I sat tight in my ravine till late that night, and suddenly in the darkness – what do you think, Azamat? – I heard a horse running along the edge of the ravine. It was snorting, neighing, stamping its hoofs – I could tell from the sound that it was my Karagyoz. It was him, my old comrade! . . . and we've never been parted since."

'I could hear him patting his horse's smooth neck and calling him various pet names.

'"If I had a thousand mares," said Azamat, "I'd give the lot for your Karagyoz."

'"*Yok*.[21] No thanks," answered Kazbich indifferently.

'"Listen, Kazbich," said Azamat, trying to get round him. "You're a good man and a brave rider, but my father fears the Russians and won't let me go into the hills. You let me have your horse and I'll do anything you want – I'll steal you my father's best rifle or sabre, anything you like. He's got a real *gurda*[22] sabre – you only have to touch the blade against your arm and it cuts into the flesh by itself – your mail shirt would be no use at all."

'Kazbich said nothing.

'"The first time I saw your horse," Azamat went on, "he was twisting and leaping under you, his nostrils flared, the flint sparks flying from his hoofs. It did something to me, I don't know what, and since then I've cared for nothing else. I despised my father's best horses – I was ashamed to be seen riding them. How miserable I was! I'd sit on the cliff for days thinking of nothing but that black horse of yours with his graceful step and sleek back, straight as an arrow. He would fix his eager eyes on mine as if he wanted to tell me something. Kazbich, I'll die if you won't sell me him," said Azamat, his voice trembling.

'I heard him burst into tears – and Azamat was an extremely stubborn lad, I might say, and nothing ever made him cry, even when he was younger.

'Kazbich answered these tears with what sounded like a laugh.

'"Listen. I'll do anything," said Azamat, his voice firm again. "What if I steal my sister for you? Think of the way she dances and sings! And the marvellous gold embroidery she does! Why, the Sultan himself never had such a wife. What do you say? Wait for me tomorrow night by the stream in the gorge. I'll take her along past there towards the next village – and she's yours! Isn't Bela worth your horse?"

'For a long time Kazbich said nothing. Then, instead of answering, he softly sang the old song:*

> Our country has many a maid that is fair,
> With eyes starry black like the midnight air.
> Happy the lad who gains love's ecstasy,
> But happier the lad whose fancy is free.
> Wives can be bought for a pot-full of gold,
> But a mettlesome steed is worth riches untold.
> He races the wind on the measureless plain,
> For ever faithful and true he'll remain.

* I beg the reader to excuse me for having put Kazbich's song into verse. It was of course given to me in prose, but habit is second nature. (M.Yu.L.)

'Azamat tried hard to persuade him, but it was no use. He wept, flattered, swore promises, till at last Kazbich lost patience and cut him short.

' "Off with you, you silly boy! How could you ride my horse? Before you'd gone a couple of yards he'd throw you and you'd crack your skull on a rock."

' "Never!" cried Azamat in fury, and I heard the boy's dagger ring against Kazbich's mail shirt. A strong arm shoved him off and he hit the fence so hard that it shook. "Now for some fun!" I thought and dashed into the stable, harnessed our horses and took them out into the back yard.

'A couple of minutes later all hell was let loose in the hut. What happened was this – Azamat went running into the hut with his *beshmet* torn and said Kazbich had tried to kill him. Everyone leapt up, grabbed their guns – and then the fun began! Shouting, yelling, guns firing. But Kazbich was already in the saddle, weaving his way along the street like a demon and beating off the crowd with his sabre.

'I caught Pechorin's arm. "No point in getting mixed up in other people's quarrels," I said. "Let's get out of here quick."

' "No, let's wait and see what happens."

' "Nothing good, you can be sure of that. These Asiatics are all the same – they get their fill of *buza*, then out come the knives!"

'We mounted and galloped home.'

'But what about Kazbich?' I asked the captain impatiently.

'His sort never come to any harm,' he replied, finishing his glass of tea. 'He got away of course.'

'Not even wounded?' I asked.

'God alone knows. Brigands like him take some killing. I've seen them in action – stuck full of bayonet holes like a sieve, but sabre still swinging.'

The captain paused for a moment, then stamped his foot and went on.

'One thing I'll never forgive myself, though. When we got

back to the fort I was fool enough to tell Pechorin what I'd heard behind the fence. He laughed, the cunning beggar. He was up to something himself.'

'What was it? Do tell me.'

'Oh, all right. Now I've started, I'd better go on.

'Three or four days after this Azamat came to the fort. He went in to see Pechorin as usual, for Pechorin always used to give him titbits to eat. I was there. They started talking about horses and Pechorin sang the praises of Kazbich's horse. It was a beauty, he said, and frisky, just like a mountain goat – in fact, the way he went on you'd have thought there was no other horse in the world like it.

'The boy's eyes glittered, but Pechorin seemed not to notice. And if I started talking about anything else he'd at once get the conversation back to Kazbich's horse. Whenever Azamat came the same thing happened. In two or three weeks I noticed the boy was looking pale and pining away like they do from love in a story-book. I couldn't understand it.

'Well, I did get to the bottom of it later – Pechorin had so teased the boy he was fit to drown himself. He said to him once: "I see that you're crazy about that horse, Azamat, but you've no more hope of getting him than you have of flying. Tell me what you'd give to anyone who got him for you."

'"Anything he liked," answered Azamat.

'"Then I'll get him for you, only on condition. Swear you'll do what I ask . . ."

'"I swear it . . . But you swear too."

'"All right, I swear you shall have the horse. But I want your sister Bela in return. Karagyoz will do as bride-money for her. I hope the deal suits you."

'Azamat said nothing.

'"You don't want to? Have it your own way then. I thought you were a man, but you're still a child, too young to be riding horses . . ."

'Azamat flared up. "What about my father?" he said.

' "Don't tell me he never goes away."

' "Yes, he does . . ."

' "Do you agree then?"

' "All right," whispered Azamat, pale as death. "But when?"

' "The next time Kazbich comes. He's promised to bring in a dozen rams. Leave the rest to me. And mind you do your part of the bargain, Azamat."

'So they fixed it up between them. A bad business it was too.

'I told Pechorin so afterwards, but he only answered that an uncivilized Circassian girl should be glad to have a nice husband like him, since, after all, according to their ways he would be her husband. And Kazbich, he said, was a brigand and deserved to be punished. I ask you, what could I say to that? . . . But at the time I didn't know about their plot. So one day Kazbich came in and asked if we wanted any rams or honey and I told him to bring some along next day. "Azamat," says Pechorin, "I'll have my hands on Karagyoz tomorrow. If Bela isn't here tonight you'll never see the horse . . ."

' "All right," said Azamat and galloped off to the village.

'That evening Pechorin armed himself and left the fort. How they fixed things I don't know, but during the night they both came back and the sentry noticed that Azamat had a woman lying across his saddle with her hands and feet tied and her head covered with a *yashmak*.'[23]

'And the horse?' I asked the captain.

'I'm just coming to that. Early next morning Kazbich turned up with a dozen rams to sell. He hitched his horse to the fence and came in to see me. I gave him some tea – for brigand though he was, we were still *kunaks*.

'We chatted about this and that and then I suddenly saw him shudder and a change come over his face. He rushed to the window, but unluckily it faced on to the back yard.

' "What's up?" I asked.

' "My horse, my horse!" he said, shaking all over.

'And in fact I did hear the clatter of hoofs.

' "It'll be some Cossack coming in . . ." I said.

' "No! *Urus yaman, yaman!*"[24] he cries, and rushes out of the house like a wild panther. In two strides he was outside. The sentry at the fort gate tried to bar his way with his gun, but he leaped over it and tore off down the road. In the distance there was a cloud of dust – Azamat galloping away on the fiery Karagyoz. Kazbich snatched his rifle from its case as he ran and fired. He stood still for a moment or two till he was sure he'd missed, then let out a wail and dashed his rifle against a stone so it broke in pieces. Then he fell to the ground and sobbed like a child. People from the fort gathered round him, but he didn't notice them. They stood and talked for a bit and then went back. I had the money for the rams put down beside him, but he didn't touch it, only lay there flat on his face as if he was dead. And believe it or not, he lay there like that the whole night through. Only next morning did he come into the fort and ask for the name of the thief. The sentry had seen Azamat untie the horse and gallop away and saw no need to keep quiet about it. At the mention of Azamat, Kazbich's eyes gleamed and he set off for the village where the boy's father lived.'

'What did the father do?'

'That was the point. He wasn't there when Kazbich turned up. He'd gone off for a few days, otherwise Azamat could never have carried off his sister.

'When the father got back he found both daughter and son gone. The boy was no fool, you see, and reckoned he'd be as good as dead if ever he was caught. He's never been heard of since. He probably joined some guerrilla band and got himself killed over the Terek or the Kuban. And jolly good riddance!

'This affair caused me some trouble too, I can tell you. As soon as I found out that the girl was in Pechorin's quarters, I put on my epaulettes and sword and went to see him.

'He was in the front room, lying on his bed with one hand under his head and the other holding a pipe that had gone out. The door of the inner room was locked and the key wasn't in the lock. I took all this in at a glance. I coughed and stamped my heels in the doorway, but he pretended not to hear.

'"Ensign Pechorin!" I said as sternly as I could. "Can't you see I'm here?"

'"Ah, hullo, Maxim Maximych. Have a pipe, won't you?" he answered, without getting up.

'"Pardon me, I am not Maxim Maximych, I'm 'sir' to you."

'"All the same, won't you have some tea? You've no idea how worried I am."

'"I know all about it," I replied, going up to his bed.

'"So much the better. I don't feel much like telling you."

'"Ensign Pechorin, you have committed an act for which I too may be held responsible."

'"Oh, come now, why all the fuss? It's always been share and share alike with us, hasn't it?"

'"What do you mean by joking, sir! Your sword, if you please!"

'"Mitka, bring my sword!"

'Mitka brought the sword. Now that I'd done my duty I sat down by him on the bed and said: "Now look here, Pechorin, this won't do, you know."

'"What won't do?"

'"Why, your taking away Bela, of course ... That rogue Azamat! Come on now, admit it," I said to him.

'"What if I like her?"

'Well, what could I say? I was at a loss. Still, after a few moments' silence I told him that if her father asked for her he'd have to give her back.

'"Nothing of the sort."

'"But what happens when he finds out she's here?"

'"How will he find out?"

'I was stumped again.

'"Look here, Maxim Maximych," said Pechorin, sitting up. "You're a kindly man. If we give that old savage back his daughter he'll slit her throat or sell her. What's done is done. There's no point in messing things up just for the fun of it. Let me keep the girl, and you're welcome to my sword . . ."

'"Show me her then," I said.

'"She's through that door, but even I couldn't see her today when I tried – she's sitting there in the corner wrapped up in her shawl and won't speak or look at you. She's as timid as a mountain goat. I've taken on the woman from the tavern – she knows Tatar and will look after her and bring her round to the idea that she belongs to me. For she'll belong to no one else!" he added, banging his fist on the table.

'I agreed again. What else could I do? There are some people you just have to agree with.'

'And what happened?' I asked Maxim Maximych. 'Did he manage to bring her round? Or did captivity make her pine away with homesickness?'

'Why should she be homesick? She saw the same mountains from the fort as she did from her village – and that's all these savages want. Besides, every day Pechorin gave her a present of some kind. The first few days she didn't say anything and proudly spurned his gifts, which went to the tavern-keeper's wife, who waxed quite eloquent about them. Ha, presents! What a woman won't do for a scrap of coloured rag! But that's another story. Pechorin had a long struggle with her. Meanwhile he learned to speak Tatar and she came to understand something of our language. She gradually came round to looking at him, secretly at first out of the corner of her eye. She was still sad though and sang songs to herself in a soft voice that made even me feel sad as I listened in the next room. I'll never forget one scene – I was walking by and happened to glance through the window. Bela was sitting on the bench by the stove, her head bowed down on her chest. Pechorin was standing in front of her.

'"Listen, my fairy," he said. "You know very well you'll be mine sooner or later, so why torment me? You're not in love with some Chechen, are you? If so, you can go home at once." She gave a faint start and shook her head. "Or do you hate me altogether?" he went on. She sighed. "Or does your religion stop you loving me?" She turned pale and said nothing. "Believe me," he said, "Allah is the same for all races and if he allows me to love you why should he stop you loving me in return?" She gazed at his face as if struck by this new thought. You could see in her eyes that she was dubious, yet wanted to believe. What eyes they were! They shone like two coals.

'"Listen, dear, sweet Bela," Pechorin went on. "You see how much I love you. I'd give anything to cheer you up. I want you to be happy, and if you're going to go on being sad then I shall die. Say that you will be more cheerful."

'She thought for a moment, her black eyes still fixed on him, then smiled sweetly and nodded her head. He took her hand and tried to get her to kiss him. She resisted feebly, just kept saying "Please, please, no, no." He became more insistent, she trembled and burst into tears. "I'm your prisoner," she said, "your slave. Of course you can make me do what you want." Then more tears.

'Pechorin struck his fist against his forehead and rushed into the next room. I went in to see him. He was walking up and down grimly, his arms folded. "What's up, old chap?" I asked him. "That's no woman, it's the devil himself," he said. "But I give you my word that she'll be mine . . ." I shook my head. "Do you want to bet?" he said. "I say she'll be mine in a week!" "By all means!" I said. We shook hands on it and parted.

'The very next day he sent a messenger off to Kizlyar²⁵ to buy various things. He came back with a vast assortment of Persian cloths, more than you could tell.

'"What do you think, Maxim Maximych," he said to me as he showed me the presents. "Will the Asian beauty hold out against a battery like this?" "You don't know Circassian women," I said. "They're nothing like Georgian women or the Transcaucasian Tatars,²⁶ nothing like that at all. They have their standards. They're brought up differently." Pechorin smiled and began whistling a march.

'As it turned out I was right. The presents did only half the trick. She grew more friendly, more trusting, but that was all. So he decided on the last resort.

'One morning he had his horse saddled, put on Circassian dress, took his weapons and went in to her. "Bela," he said, "you know how much I love you. I decided to carry you off thinking you would come to love me when you got to know me. I was wrong. Good-bye. All I have is yours to keep. Go back to your father if you want – you're free. I've done you wrong and must punish myself. Good-bye. I'm going away. Where I'll go I don't know. I don't suppose it will be long before I can find death from a bullet or sabre-stroke. Remember me then and forgive me."

'He turned away and offered his hand in parting. She didn't take it or say anything. But from where I was behind the door I could see her face through the crack. I pitied her to see how deathly pale that sweet little face had gone. Hearing no answer, Pechorin took a few steps towards the door. He was trembling, and I might say I think he was fit to do what he'd threatened as a joke. That's the sort of man he was, there was no knowing him. But he'd hardly touched the door when she sprang up sobbing and threw her arms around his neck. Believe it or not, but I wept myself as I stood there behind the door. Well, not exactly wept, you know – oh, just an old man's silliness!'

The captain was silent.

'Yes,' he said, tugging at his whiskers, 'I confess I was upset that no woman had ever loved me like that.'

'Did their happiness last long?' I asked.

'Yes, she admitted to us that after she first saw Pechorin she had often dreamt of him and that no man had ever made her feel that way before. Yes, they were happy.'

'How dull!' I found myself exclaiming.

There was I expecting some tragic end only to have my hopes dashed in this unexpected fashion!

'Do you mean to say her father had no idea you'd got her in the fort?' I asked.

'Well, actually I think he did suspect it, but a few days later we heard the old man had been killed. It was like this . . .'

I was once more all attention.

'Kazbich, you see, had got the idea that the old man had connived at Azamat's stealing his horse. That's what I reckon, anyway. So one night he lay in wait for him on the road a mile or two from the village. The old man had been out trying to find his daughter and was on his way home. It was just getting dark. He'd got ahead of his men and was walking his horse, thinking things over. All of a sudden Kazbich springs out like a cat from behind a bush, jumps up on the horse behind him and fells him with his dagger. Then he grabs the reins and is gone. Some of the men saw all this from the hill above. They dashed after him but couldn't catch him.'

'So he got his revenge and made up for the loss of his horse,' I said, hoping to elicit my companion's opinion.

'Of course, to their way of thinking he was quite right,' said the captain.

I couldn't help being struck by this capacity of Russians to adapt themselves to the ways of peoples they happen to live among. I don't know if this is a praiseworthy quality or not, but it does show wonderful flexibility and that clear common sense that can forgive evil wherever it is seen to be inevitable or ineradicable.

Meanwhile, we had finished our tea. The horses had long been harnessed and were chilled through in the snow. In the west a pale moon was about to sink into the black clouds that hung like tattered shreds of curtain on the distant peaks. We left the hut. The weather had cleared, in spite of what my companion had said, and a fine morning promised. Far away on the horizon groups of dancing stars wove wondrous patterns, fading one by one as the pale light of dawn spread over the deep violet sky and lit up the virgin snow on the steep mountain slopes. Dark mysterious chasms yawned on either side of us. Wreaths of mist coiled and twisted like snakes, sliding down the folds of neighbouring cliffs into the abyss, as though they sensed and feared the approach of day. There was peace in heaven and on earth. It was like the heart of a man at morning prayer. Only occasionally a puff of cool easterly breeze ruffled the horses' frosty manes.

We set off. Five lean nags toiled up the winding road towards Gud-Gora with our carts, while we followed on foot, wedging stones under the wheels when the horses were winded. The road seemed to lead right up to the sky, for it went on rising as far as the eye could see, to vanish in the cloud that had rested on Gud-Gora since the day before, like a kite awaiting its prey.

Snow crunched beneath our feet. The air was getting so thin that it hurt to breathe. The blood kept rushing to one's head. Yet for all that every fibre of my body tingled with ecstasy. I felt somehow happy to be so high above the world – a childish feeling, I grant, but we can't help becoming children as we leave social conventions behind and come nearer to nature. All life's experience is shed from us and the soul becomes anew what it once was and will surely be again.

Anyone who has chanced like me to roam through desolate mountains and studied at length their fantastic shapes and drunk the invigorating air of their valleys can understand why I wish to describe and depict these magic scenes for others.

At long last we reached the top of Gud-Gora. We stopped and looked round. A grey cloud hung over the mountain. Its chilly breath threatened an imminent storm, but the sky was so clear and golden to the east that the captain and I never gave it a thought. No, not even the captain, for a simple man feels nature's beauty and grandeur a hundred times more powerfully and keenly than rapturous story-tellers like me who write and talk about these things.

'You're used to this splendid scenery, I suppose,' I said.

'Oh, yes. Of course, you can even get used to bullets whistling past you – used, that is, to hiding the pounding of your heart.'

'I've heard, though, that many old soldiers find it music in their ears.'

26

'Well, yes, all right, you can even enjoy it. But only because your heart beats faster. Look,' he said, pointing towards the east. 'What a marvellous place this is!'

And sure enough, I'm hardly likely to see such a view again. Below us lay the Koyshaur Valley with the Aragva and some lesser river crossing it like two silver threads. Bluish mist drifted down the valley, sheltering in the neighbouring gorges from the warmth of the morning sun. To right and left stretched intersecting chains of snowy, scrub-covered mountains, towering one above the other. There were still more mountains in the distance, though never two cliffs alike. And everywhere the snow shone with a ruddy glow, looking so bright and gay that one felt like staying and living there for ever. The sun peeped over the top of a deep blue mountain that only a practised eye could tell from a thunder cloud. A bloody streak lay over the sun and my companion eyed it with special interest.

'I told you we were in for a storm today,' he declared. 'We'd better hurry up or we'll get caught on the Krestovaya. Get moving!' he shouted to the drivers.

They put chains under the wheels to act as a brake to stop them running away, took the horses by the bridle and began the descent. On the right was sheer cliff and on the left a chasm so deep that an Ossete village at the bottom looked no bigger than a swallow's nest. I shuddered when I thought of the couriers who pass this way a dozen times a year. The road at this point is too narrow for two carts to pass, yet they go down it at dead of night and never even bother to get out of their jolting carriages.

One of our drivers was a Russian peasant from Yaroslavl, the other an Ossete. The Ossete unharnessed the leading pair and led the shaft horse by the bridle, going very warily. Yet all this time our good Russian blithely kept his seat on the box! I pointed out to him that he might at least spare a thought for my portmanteau, as I wasn't all that keen on scrambling after it into the ravine.

'Never you worry, sir,' he said. 'With God's grace we'll get there just the same as them. After all, we've done it before.'

And he was right. True, we might never have arrived, but the fact is we did. If only people thought a little more about it, they would see that life is not worth worrying about so much.

But perhaps you want to know how the story of Bela ended? First, though, I must remind you that I am writing travel notes, not a story, and so I cannot make the captain tell his tale before he in fact did so. You must therefore wait or, if you prefer, turn on a few pages – though I would advise you not to do this, for the crossing of the Krestovaya (or Mont Saint-Christophe, as the learned Gamba calls it)[27] is well worth your attention.

We descended then from Gud-Gora into Chertova Valley.[28] A romantic name! You picture to yourself the lair of the Evil One set among inaccessible crags. But you are wrong – the name Chertova does not come from *chert* 'devil', but from *cherta* 'boundary', for this was once the Georgian frontier. The valley was blocked with snowdrifts that brought back vivid memories of Saratov, Tambov[29] and other such endearing parts of our native land.

We completed our descent.

'There's the Krestovaya,' said the captain, pointing to a snow-covered hill with a black cross on its summit. By the cross one could just make out the road, which is only used when the road skirting the hill is blocked with snow. Our drivers said there had not been any avalanches yet, so they took us by the side road to spare the horses.

At a turning we met half a dozen Ossetes who offered us their services. They seized the wheels and with much shouting set to pulling and steadying our carts. The road was certainly dangerous. On our right were piles of overhanging snow, looking as though the first gust of wind would send them plunging into the ravine. The narrow road was partly covered with snow. In some places it gave way under our feet, but in others it had been turned into ice by the sun and the night frost. We found the going difficult enough ourselves; our horses kept stumbling. On our left yawned a deep chasm down which a torrent flowed, one moment vanishing beneath the crust of ice, the next leaping and foaming over black rocks.

We barely managed to get round the Krestovaya in two hours. Two hours to cover a mile and a half! Meanwhile the clouds came down and it began hailing and snowing hard. The wind tore through the ravines, roaring and whistling like the Robber Solovey[30] in the folk-tale. The stone cross was soon lost in the banks of mist that rolled in ever thicker and faster from the east.

There is, by the way, a strange, though widespread legend about this cross. It is said to have been put up by Peter the First[31] as he was crossing the Caucasus. But, in the first place, Peter only went to Daghestan; and in the second place, it says on the cross in large letters that it was erected by order of General Yermolov, in 1824 to be exact. But in spite of this inscription, the legend is so well established that you do not know what to believe, especially as we are not used to believing what we read on inscriptions anyway.

We had to go down another three and a half miles over ice-covered cliffs and soft snow to reach the station at Kobi.[32] The horses were dead beat and we were absolutely frozen. The blizzard howled more and more furiously. It might have been one of our storms back home in the north, though its wild refrains were sadder, more doleful.

You too are an exile, I thought. You mourn for the broad open steppes where you have room to spread your icy wings. Here you feel stifled and constricted, like an eagle that cries and beats against the bars of its iron cage.

'I don't like it,' said the captain. 'Look at it. You can't see a thing. Nothing but snow and mist. We'll be over a cliff or stuck in a gulley if we don't watch out. Then farther down we'll very likely find the Baidara[33] in full spate, so we shan't get across. Asia! What a place! The people and the rivers are as bad as each other – there's no depending on 'em.'

The drivers shouted and swore as they whipped the horses,

which snorted and held back. They would not budge for anything, for all the eloquence of the whips.

At last one driver said:

'We'll never make Kobi today, sir. Shall we turn off to the left while we still can? There's something over there on the hillside. Must be huts. Travellers always put up here in bad weather.' He pointed to an Ossete. 'They say they'll take us there if you give them a tip.'

'I know, lad, I don't need you to tell me,' said the captain. 'Lord, what swine! They never miss a chance to pick up a tip.'

'Still, you must admit we'd be worse off without them,' I said.

'I know, I know,' he muttered. 'Huh! Guides! They know which side their bread's buttered. Making out you can't find the way without them to help!'

So we turned off to the left and after a good deal of trouble reached our humble shelter. It consisted of two huts built of flat stones and rubble, enclosed by a wall of the same material. Our ragged hosts gave us a warm welcome. I learnt afterwards that they are paid and kept by the government on condition they take in travellers caught by storms.

I sat down by the fire.

'It's all to the good,' I said. 'Now you can finish your story about Bela. I'm sure that wasn't the end of it.'

'What makes you so sure?' asked the captain, winking and smiling artfully.

'Why, it's not in the nature of things. An unusual beginning must have an unusual end.'

'As a matter of fact you're right.'

'Good.'

'It's all very well for you to be pleased. It's sad for me, though, to look back on it. She was a grand girl, was Bela. I got so attached to her, I loved her like a daughter. She was fond of me too. I have no family, you know. It's twelve years or more since I heard anything of my father and mother. I never thought of taking a wife earlier on and now at my age it wouldn't be proper. So I was glad to have someone to make a fuss of. She used to sing songs for us or dance the *lezginka*.[34] Some dancer she was too. I've seen our young ladies in the provinces, and once, twenty years back, I even went to the Assembly Rooms in Moscow[35] – but those girls weren't a patch on Bela. She was in a different class altogether. Pechorin dressed her up like a doll, and it was amazing how much prettier she grew while with us, with all his pampering and coddling. She lost the sunburn on her face and arms and got some colour in her cheeks. A gay spark she was, always teasing me, the little imp . . . God forgive her.'

'And what happened when you told her her father was dead?'

'We kept it from her for a long time. Then when she was used to being with us we told her. She cried for a couple of days, then forgot all about it.

'Everything was fine for three or four months. I think I told you Pechorin was very keen on hunting. He'd a regular passion for it, always out in the forest after wild-boar or goats. But now he never so much as went outside the ramparts. Soon, though, I saw he was brooding again, walking round the room with his hands behind his back. Then one day he went off shooting without saying a word to anybody. He was gone the whole morning. It happened once, then again. Then more and more often. Something's up, I thought. They've had a tiff.

'I went in to see them one morning. I can see it now – Bela sitting on the bed in a black silk *beshmet* and looking that pale and sad it gave me quite a turn.

'"Where's Pechorin?" I said.

'"Hunting."

'"Did he go off this morning?"

'She said nothing. She seemed to find it hard to talk. In the end she gave a deep sigh and said:

'"No, he went yesterday."

'"You don't suppose anything has happened to him?" I said.

'She answered through her tears.

'"All day yesterday I was thinking, imagining all kinds of

accidents. One moment I thought he'd been wounded by a boar, then that he'd been carried off to the hills by some Chechen. But now I think he doesn't love me any more."

'"Truly, my dear, that's the worst possible thing you could think."

'She burst into tears. Then she proudly lifted her head and wiped her eyes.

'"If he doesn't love me," she said, "why can't he send me home? I'm not forcing him to keep me. I'll go myself if it goes on like this. I'm not his slave, I'm a chief's daughter."

'I tried to talk her round.

'"Look, Bela," I said. "You can't expect him to spend his whole time here tied to your apron-strings. He's a young man and fond of the chase. He'll go off hunting, then come back. But if you're going to mope, he'll soon get tired of you."

'"Yes, you're right," she said. "I'll cheer up."

'She laughed and took her tambourine and started to sing and dance and leap around me. But this didn't last long either. She fell on to the bed again and covered her face with her hands.

'What could I do with her? You see, I'd never had any dealings with women. I racked my brains for some way of comforting her, but I couldn't think of anything. For some time neither of us spoke. Very awkward it was.

'In the end I asked if she would like a walk to the ramparts, as the weather was fine. It was September and a really lovely day, bright but not too hot. The mountains all round were as clear as anything. We set off and walked along the ramparts for a long time, saying nothing. At last she sat down on the grass with me beside her. It's really funny to look back on – there was I fussing over her like a nursemaid.

'Our fort stood on high ground, with a magnificent view from the ramparts. On one side was a broad stretch of open country with gullies running across it, and forest beyond stretching right up to the mountains. Here and there you'd see smoke from the villages, and herds of horses moving about. On the other side there was a shallow stream, bordered by the thick scrub of the stony mountains that link up with the main Caucasus range.

'We sat on the corner of the bastion, with a good view in both directions. Suddenly I saw a man on a grey horse coming out of the wood. He came closer and closer, then stopped on the far side of the stream a couple of hundred yards away. He was wheeling his horse round like a madman. I couldn't understand what he was up to.

'"Your eyes are younger than mine, Bela," I said. "Can you see who that rider is? Who's he putting on that show for?"

'She had a look and shrieked:

'"It's Kazbich!"

'"The scoundrel!" I cried. "Come to make sport of us, has he?"

'I had a good look. It was Kazbich sure enough, the black-faced scoundrel, as tattered and filthy as ever.

'"That's my father's horse!" said Bela, grasping my arm. She was trembling like a leaf, her eyes flashing.

'"Ho, ho!" I thought. "The brigand's blood's coming out in you as well, my sweetheart!"

'I called the sentry.

'"Come here," I said. "Check your gun and pick me off that fellow down there. There's a silver rouble for you if you do."

'"Very good, sir," says he. "But he don't keep still."

'"You tell him to," I laughed.

'So the sentry waved to him and shouted:

'"Hold still a minute, friend. What are you up to, spinning round like a top?"

'Kazbich stopped and listened – he must have thought we wanted to parley. But he had another think coming to him! My grenadier took aim and fired. He missed. The moment the powder flashed in the pan, Kazbich spurred his horse and it leapt to one side. He stood up in the stirrups and shouted something in his own language, then shook his whip at us and was gone.

'"You ought to be ashamed of yourself," I told the sentry.

' "He's gone off to die, sir," he said. "These damned people, you can't kill 'em straight off."

'A quarter of an hour later Pechorin came back from hunting. Bela threw her arms round his neck with never a murmur of complaint or reproach about his being away so long.

'Even I was annoyed with him.

' "Look here," I said. "Kazbich was just across the river a minute ago and we took a shot at him. You might easily have bumped into him. These hillmen don't take things lying down. Do you think he doesn't guess you had a hand in helping Azamat? And I'll bet he recognized Bela just now. He was very keen on her a year ago – I know that for a fact, for he told me so himself. If he'd seen his way to raising the bride-money, he'd have asked for her hand, for sure."

'This made Pechorin think.

' "Yes," he said. "We must be more careful. Bela, from now on you must never go out on the ramparts again."

'I had a long talk with him that evening. It vexed me to see the way he'd changed towards the poor girl. Apart from spending half his time out hunting, he treated her coldly now and rarely made a fuss of her. You could see she was beginning to pine. Her face was drawn and the sparkle had gone from her great big eyes. I'd say to her: "What are you sighing for, Bela? Feeling sad?" "No," she'd say. "Is there something you want?" "No." "Are you missing your family?" "I have no family." Sometimes you'd get nothing out of her for days on end but just "Yes" and "No".

'This was what I talked to Pechorin about.

' "Look, Maxim Maximych," he said. "I've got an unfortunate character. I don't know how I came by it, whether it was the way I was brought up or whether it's just the way I'm made. All I know is that if I make other people unhappy, I'm no less unhappy myself. Not much comfort for them perhaps, but there it is. As a young man, as soon as I got my freedom I threw myself wildly into all the pleasures that money can buy, and soon grew sick of them, needless to say. Then I went in for society high-life and

BLASÉ

before long I was tired of that too. I fell in love with women of fashion and was loved in return. But their love merely stirred my imagination and vanity, my heart remained empty. I took to reading and study, but grew tired of that too. I saw I had no need of learning to win fame or happiness, for the happiest people are the ignoramuses, and fame is a matter of luck and you only need to be smart to get it. I got bored after that.

'"Soon after, I was posted to the Caucasus. That was the happiest time in my life. I hoped there'd be an end to boredom with Chechen bullets flying around, but I was wrong. After a month I was so used to the hum of bullets and to being close to death that I honestly took more notice of the mosquitoes. Now I was more bored than ever, with just about my last hope gone. When I saw Bela in my quarters and held her on my knees and kissed her black curls for the first time I was silly enough to think she was an angel sent down to me by a merciful fate. I was wrong again. A native girl's love is little better than that of a lady of rank. The ignorance and simplicity of the one are as tiresome as the coquetry of the other. If you like, I'm still in love with her. I'm grateful to her for a few moments of relative bliss. I'd give my life for her. But she bores me. I don't know whether I'm a fool or a scoundrel, but one thing I am sure of is that I'm just as much to be pitied as she is, perhaps even more. My soul's been corrupted by society. My imagination knows no peace, my heart no satisfaction. Nothing counts for me. I grow used to sorrow as easily as I do to pleasure, and my life gets emptier every day. The only thing left for me is to travel. As soon as I can I'll leave. Not for Europe, though, not on your life. I'll go to America, Arabia, India. Perhaps I'll die somewhere on the way. At least I can be sure that with storms and bad roads to help this final solace will last me a while."

'He talked a long time in this vein. What he said made a deep impression on me, for it was the first time I'd ever heard such things from a man of twenty-five, and God grant it may be the last. It's quite beyond me. Now you're a man who's lately been in the capital,' he said, looking at me. 'Is it true that all the young people there are the same?'

I said there were a lot of people who did talk like that and very likely some of them told the truth, but disenchantment, like any other fashion, having started off among the élite had now been passed down to finish its days among the lower orders. I explained that now the people who suffered most from boredom tried to keep their misfortune to themselves, as if it were some vice.

The captain could not understand these subtleties. He shook his head.

'I suppose it was the French who started this fashion of being bored?' he said, smiling artfully.

'No, the English.'

'Aha, so that's it! They always were a drunken lot,' he retorted. I could not help recalling the Moscow lady who used to maintain that Byron was no more than a drunkard. But the captain had more excuse for talking this way, since, being anxious to keep off alcohol, he naturally tried to persuade himself that drunkenness was the cause of all the world's misfortunes.

Meanwhile he continued his story.

'Kazbich didn't show up again. Still, for some reason I couldn't get rid of the idea that he'd come for a purpose and was up to some devilry.

'One day Pechorin tried to get me to go boar-hunting with him. I put him off for a long time – really, as if I cared about wild boar! But in the end he got me to go with him, and we set off first thing in the morning with half a dozen soldiers. We routed about in the forest and among the reeds till ten o'clock, but found no boar.

'"We may as well go back," I said. "What's the point of keeping on? It's plain we're out of luck today."

'But Pechorin wasn't for going back empty-handed, no matter about the heat and being tired. He was like that. He'd get something into his head and not be content till he got it. He must have been spoilt as a child. At midday we did at last come on a

confounded boar and got in a couple of shots, but it was no good
– he got away among the reeds. It just wasn't our day. So we had
a bit of a rest and set off home.

'We rode side by side in silence, trailing our reins, and we'd
almost reached the fort – it was just out of sight behind some
bushes – when we heard a shot. We looked at each other, both
seized with the same suspicion, and galloped full tilt to where the
shot had come from. We saw a group of soldiers gathered on the
ramparts and pointing out across the plain. There was a horseman
going like the wind, with something white across the saddle.
Pechorin let out a shriek as good as any Chechen, grabbed his
gun from the holster and was after him like a shot, with me
following behind.

'As luck had it, our horses were still fresh, as we'd seen little
sport, and they went flat out. Every second we got closer. Then
at last I saw it was Kazbich, though I couldn't make out what he
was holding in front of him. I came level with Pechorin and
shouted to him that it was Kazbich. He glanced at me, nodded
and whipped up his horse.

'At length we got within range. Perhaps Kazbich's horse was
tired or just not as good as ours, anyway for all his efforts it wasn't
making much ground. I fancy Kazbich must have thought back
to his Karagyoz just then.

'I saw Pechorin take aim at the gallop. "Don't fire," I shouted.
"Save your shot. We'll catch him anyway." But young people are
all the same – they always get carried away at the wrong moment.
There was a shot, and the bullet got Kazbich's horse in the back
leg. In the heat of the moment it bounded on another dozen steps,
then stumbled and fell on its knees. Kazbich jumped off and we
saw then that he was carrying a woman wrapped in a *yashmak*. It
was Bela, poor thing.

'Kazbich shouted something to us in his own language and
lifted a dagger over her. There was no time to waste. I fired my
shot without taking aim and must have got him in the shoulder,
for suddenly he dropped his arm. When the smoke cleared I saw

the wounded horse lying on the ground with Bela by its side. Kazbich had thrown away his gun and was scrambling like a cat through the bushes up a crag. I'd have liked to bring him down from there, but my gun needed reloading. We jumped off our horses and rushed to Bela. Poor soul, she lay quite still, with blood streaming from her wound. That villain Kazbich couldn't stab her clean in the heart and get it over with, he had to stab her in the back like the brigand he was.

'She was unconscious. We tore up her *yashmak* and tied up the wound as tight as we could. Pechorin kissed her cold lips in vain. Nothing could bring her round.

'Pechorin mounted while I lifted her up and somehow we managed to get her on to his saddle. He put his arms round her and we started back. We said nothing for a few minutes, then Pechorin spoke.

' "Look, Maxim Maximych, we'll never get her back alive like this."

'I agreed, so we galloped as fast as we could go. There was a crowd to meet us at the fort gate. We carried her carefully across to Pechorin's quarters and sent for the doctor, who was drunk, but came just the same. He looked at the wound and said she wouldn't last more than a day. He was wrong, though . . .'

'Did she get better then?' I asked the captain, seizing him by the arm. I could not help being pleased.

'No,' he said. 'The doctor was wrong because in fact she lived for two days.'

'How did Kazbich manage to get her away then?' I asked.

'It was like this. Although Pechorin had told her not to, she went out of the fort down to the stream. It was very hot, you see, so she sat down on a stone and dangled her feet in the water. Kazbich sneaked up, grabbed her, put his hand over her mouth and pulled her into the bushes. Then he was up in the saddle and off. She meantime managed to let out a shout and rouse the sentries. They fired, but missed, and that's when we turned up.'

'But why did Kazbich want to take her away?'

'Why, what do you think? These Circassians have got thieving in their blood. They'll steal anything, given the chance. Even things they don't want – they'll take them just the same. They just can't help it. And besides he'd long had a fancy for her.'

'Bela died then?'

'Yes, she died, though she suffered a long time. And we suffered our fill along with her. About ten that evening she came round. We sat by her bed. The moment she opened her eyes she called for Pechorin.

'"I'm here by your side, my *dzhanechka* (my darling, that is, in our language)," he said and took her hand.

'"I'm going to die," she said.

'We comforted her, told her the doctor had promised to make her better without fail, but she shook her head and turned to the wall. She didn't want to die.

'In the night she became delirious. Her head was burning and every so often her whole body shook with fever. She rambled on about her father and her brother, and said she wanted to go home to the mountains. Then she talked about Pechorin too, called him all kinds of affectionate names or else reproached him for no longer loving his *dzhanechka*.

'He listened to her, without a word, resting his head on his hands. All this time, though, I never once saw a tear in his eye. Perhaps he couldn't cry, perhaps he controlled himself, I don't know. As far as I was concerned, I'd never seen anything so pathetic in my life.

'By morning the delirium had passed. She lay still for an hour or so. She was pale and so weak you could hardly tell she was breathing. Then she improved and started talking. Do you know what about? It was the kind of fancy that only comes to people when they are dying. She said she felt sad that she wasn't a Christian and that her spirit would never meet Pechorin's in the next world and some other woman would be his sweetheart in heaven. I thought of getting her baptized before she died and suggested it to her. She looked at me, not sure what to do. She couldn't speak for a long time, but in the end said she'd die in the faith she'd been born in.

'The whole day passed like this. What a change came over her in that one day! Her cheeks were pale and sunken, her eyes enormous, her lips afire. She had a burning pain, like a red hot iron in her breast.

'The next night came. We never shut an eye and stayed by her bed the whole time. She was groaning and in terrible agony. When the pain let up she tried to make Pechorin think she felt better, told him to go to bed, kissed his hand and wouldn't let it go.

'Just before dawn she started to feel the anguish of death. She tossed and turned, the bandage came off and she started bleeding again. We tied up the wound and she was quiet for a minute and asked Pechorin to kiss her. He knelt by the bed, raised her head from the pillow and pressed his lips to hers, from which the warmth was already passing. She hugged him tight round the neck, her arms trembling, as though she was trying to pass her soul to him with that kiss. No, it was right and proper she should die! What would have become of her if Pechorin had left her, as he would have done sooner or later?

'Half the next day she was quiet, saying nothing, and doing all she was told, however much the doctor tormented her with his poultices and medicine.

'"Look here," I told him. "You said yourself she's bound to die, so why bother with all these concoctions of yours?"

'"It's better this way," he says. "I must keep a clear conscience."

'Conscience, my foot!

'That afternoon she was tormented with thirst. We opened the window, but it was hotter outside than in. We put ice by the bed, but it was no use. I knew this frantic thirst was a sign that the end was near and told Pechorin so. Bela raised herself on the bed and called out hoarsely for water. Pechorin turned white as a sheet, snatched up a glass, poured some water and gave it her. I put my hands over my eyes and said a prayer, which one I don't remember. Yes, sir, I've seen plenty of people dying in hospitals and on the battlefield, but this was something different, altogether different. Truth to tell, it still grieves me that she never once remembered me as she lay dying, though I think I loved her like a father. Well, God forgive her ... And after all, who am I that people should think of me when they're dying?

'The moment she drank the water she felt better, but then two or three minutes later she passed away. We put a mirror to her lips and it didn't blur. I took Pechorin out of the room and we went to the ramparts. We walked up and down for a long time, our hands behind our backs, saying nothing. His face showed nothing in particular, and that annoyed me. If I'd been in his place I'd have died of grief. In the end he sat on the ground in some shade and started drawing in the sand with a stick. I wanted to console him, more for decency's sake, you understand, than anything else. But when I spoke he lifted up his head and laughed. That laugh sent cold shivers down my spine.

'I went off to order the coffin. I confess it was partly to occupy my mind that I saw to this. I lined the coffin with a piece of Persian silk I had and trimmed it round with some silver Circassian lace that Pechorin had bought for Bela.

'Early next morning we buried her near the spot where she had last sat, outside the fort by the stream. White acacias and elder have grown up round her grave now. I wanted to put up a cross, but didn't like to somehow. After all, she wasn't a Christian.'

'What about Pechorin?' I asked.

'Poor chap. He was out of sorts for a long time and got very thin. But we never talked of Bela after that. I could see it would upset him, so what was the point? Three or four months later he was posted to another regiment and went off to Georgia, and I've not heard of him since then. I seem to remember somebody told me recently he'd gone back to Russia, though there was nothing about it in divisional orders. But then, the likes of us are always the last to get the news.'

At this point he launched into a lengthy discourse on the inconveniences of hearing news a year after the event. Probably he wanted to suppress his sad memories. I did not interrupt him, nor did I listen.

In an hour it was possible to move on. The storm had abated, the sky had cleared, and we set off. As we journeyed I could not help bringing up the subject of Bela and Pechorin again.

'Did you never hear what happened to Kazbich?' I asked.

'Kazbich? No, I don't rightly know. I've heard tell the Shapsugs on the right flank have got a daredevil fellow called Kazbich[36] – he wears a red *beshmet*, and whenever he comes under our fire he just walks his horse up and down, and bows very civil every time a bullet whistles by. But it can hardly be the same one.'

At Kobi, Maxim Maximych and I parted company. I travelled on by post chaise, and he, with his heavy baggage, could not keep up with me. We never expected to meet again, but in fact we did. If you like I will tell you about it – it is quite a story. Don't you agree, though, that Maxim Maximych is a sterling fellow? If you do, then I shall be amply rewarded for my – perhaps too lengthy – tale.

II

Maxim Maximych

After leaving Maxim Maximych I travelled briskly through the
Terek and Daryal gorges, lunched at Kazbek, had tea at Lars and
arrived in Vladikavkaz[1] in time for supper. But I won't burden
you with descriptions of mountains, meaningless exclamations of
rapture, depictions of scenery which convey nothing, least of all
to anyone who has never been there, and statistics which no one
would ever read.

I put up at the hotel where travellers always stay and where, I
might mention, it's impossible to get a pheasant roasted or a drop
of soup cooked, because the three old soldiers in charge of it are
too stupid or too drunk to do a thing.

I was told I would have to spend another three days there since
the 'detachment' had not yet arrived from Yekaterinograd[2] and
was therefore in no position to return. I did not view that with
detachment! However, a bad pun is small comfort for a Russian,
and I decided to pass the time by writing down Maxim Maximych's
story of Bela. Little did I think it would be the first of a whole
series of tales. It just goes to show what terrible consequences a
trivial incident can have.

But you may not know what a 'detachment' is? It is an escort
– half a company of infantry and one cannon – that accompanies
convoys passing through Kabarda on their way from Vladikavkaz
to Yekaterinograd.

My first day there was very tedious. Early next morning a cart
drove into the yard, and who should it be but Maxim Maximych!

We greeted each other like long lost friends. I gave him the use of my room. He did not stand on ceremony and even went so far as to slap me on the back and curl his lips in an apology for a smile. What a strange fellow he is!

Maxim Maximych was well versed in the culinary arts and produced a remarkably good roast pheasant, nicely dressed with a cucumber sauce. I must admit that but for him I should have had to make do with hard tack. A bottle of Kakhetian wine[3] helped us to forget the modest number of courses (one in all), and after dinner we lit our pipes and settled ourselves, I by the window, Maxim Maximych by the stove, which had been lit as the day was damp and cold.

We sat in silence. What was there to talk about? He had already told me all there was of interest about himself and I, for my part, had nothing to tell. I looked out of the window. Through the trees I glimpsed numerous small houses dotted along the bank of the Terek, which gets steadily wider all the time. Beyond lay the jagged blue wall of mountains, with the white cardinal's cap of Kazbek[4] peeping out behind. I was sorry to be leaving them and bade them a mental farewell.

We sat like this for a long time. The sun dipped behind the cold mountain peaks and a whitish mist began to spread through the valleys. Suddenly there was the sound of a carriage bell and the shout of coachmen outside. Some carts of filthy Armenians drove into the hotel yard, followed by an empty calash. Its light undercarriage, comfortable fittings and dandyish appearance had a foreign stamp about them. A servant walked behind. He wore large mustachios and a braided jacket and was rather well-dressed for a servant, but the devil-may-care flourish with which he knocked out his pipe and the way he shouted at the driver left one in no doubt as to his station in life. He was clearly the pampered servant of a lazy master, a kind of Russian Figaro.[5] I called to him from the window.

'I say, my man! Is that the detachment arrived?'

He gave me a rather insolent look, straightened his neckband

and turned away. An Armenian walking beside him smiled and answered for him. It was the detachment, he said, and it would be going back the next morning.

'Thank heavens for that!' said Maxim Maximych, who had joined me at the window. 'Why, that's a mighty fine carriage!' he added. 'Must be some official on his way to Tiflis for an inquiry. You can see he doesn't know much about the hills in these parts. They're cruel they are, make no mistake. Even an English carriage wouldn't stand up to them.'

'I wonder who it can be,' I said. 'Let's go and find out.'

We went out into the passage. At the far end a door leading to a side room was open. The servant and the driver were carrying cases into it.

'Here, fellow!' said Maxim Maximych to the servant. 'Whose is that splendid calash out there, eh? It's a fine job.'

Without turning, the servant muttered something under his breath as he untied a portmanteau. Maxim Maximych was annoyed and touched the churlish fellow on the shoulder.

'Here, I'm speaking to you, my man . . .' he said.

'Whose calash? It's my master's.'

'And who's your master?'

'Pechorin . . .'

'What's that? Pechorin? Why, good heavens above!' exclaimed Maxim Maximych, tugging my sleeve. 'Did your master ever see service in the Caucasus?' he asked, his eyes shining with joy.

'Yes, I think he did. I've not been with him long,' said the servant.

'That's it, that's it! Grigory Alexandrovich – that's his name, isn't it? I was a friend of your master's,' he said, giving the servant a friendly slap on the shoulder that sent him staggering.

The servant frowned.

'If you please, sir. You're holding me up,' he said.

'Heavens above, fellow! You don't seem to realize – we were bosom friends, your master and I. Shared quarters, we did. But where's your master got to?'

The servant explained that Pechorin was dining and spending the night at the house of Colonel N.

'Do you think he'll be coming round here this evening?' asked Maxim Maximych. 'Or perhaps you'll have to go and see him about something? If you do, tell him Maxim Maximych is here. Just say that, he'll know . . . There'll be an eighty-copek piece for you.'

The servant gave a look of disdain on hearing this modest promise. Still, he told Maxim Maximych he would do as he asked.

'You see. He'll be round at once,' Maxim Maximych told me with a triumphant look. 'I'll go and wait for him outside the gate. What a pity I don't know N.'

Maxim Maximych sat down on the bench outside the gate and I went back to my room. I confess I also awaited with some impatience the appearance of this man Pechorin. The impression I had gained of him from the captain's story was not a specially favourable one, but some features of his character had struck me as remarkable.

An hour passed. One of the old soldiers brought in a boiling *samovar*[6] and a teapot.

I shouted to Maxim Maximych out of the window.

'Maxim Maximych! Will you have some tea?'

'No, thanks very much,' he said. 'I don't feel like any just now.'

'Come on, have some. The time's getting on, and it's chilly.'

'I'm all right, thanks very much.'

'Very well. Please yourself.'

I started on the tea by myself. Ten minutes later in came my old friend.

'You're right,' he said. 'A drop of tea would be best, after all. I've been waiting all this time. His servant went to see him a long time ago, but he must have got held up.'

He quickly gulped down a cup of tea, refused a second and went off to the gate again, looking upset. The old fellow was clearly hurt by Pechorin's indifference, particularly as he had just been telling me what great friends they were and an hour ago had been sure Pechorin would rush to see him at the mere mention of his name.

It was already late and dark when I next opened the window and called Maxim Maximych to tell him it was bedtime. He muttered something through his teeth, and when I repeated the invitation he made no reply.

I left a candle on the bench by the stove, wrapped myself in my greatcoat and lay down on the couch. I soon dozed off and would have slept peacefully through till morning, if Maxim Maximych had not woken me. He came in very late, threw his pipe on the table, paced up and down the room, tinkered with the stove, and when he finally did go to bed, he coughed, spat and tossed and turned for a long time.

'Bedbugs troubling you?' I asked.

He gave a deep sigh.

'Yes, that's it,' he said.

I woke early in the morning, but Maxim Maximych was up before me. I found him sitting on the bench by the gate.

'I've got to call on the commandant,' he said. 'So would you send round for me if Pechorin turns up?'

I promised I would, and he ran off as though his limbs had regained all the vigour and suppleness of youth.

It was a beautiful morning, though fresh. Golden clouds massed on the mountains like some new range of aerial peaks. Outside the gate there was a broad square, with a market on the far side. As it was Sunday the market was bustling with people, and barefooted Ossete boys swarmed round me with baskets of honey-combs on their backs. I sent them packing. I had other thoughts, for I was beginning to share the concern of the good captain.

Within ten minutes the man we awaited appeared at the end of the square with Colonel N. The colonel accompanied him as far as the hotel, then said good-bye and turned to go back to the fort. I at once sent one of the old soldiers to fetch Maxim Maximych.

Pechorin's servant came out of the hotel to meet him and said that the horses would be harnessed at once; he handed him a cigar-box and Pechorin gave some instructions which the servant went off to attend to. His master lit a cigar, yawned a couple of times and sat down on the bench on the far side of the gate.

I must now give you a portrait of him.

He was of average height, with broad shoulders and a slender shapely figure that indicated a strong physique, capable of enduring the rigours of a wandering life and changes in climate, and proof against the turmoil of passions and the corruption of city life. His dusty velvet coat was undone, except for the two bottom buttons, and an expanse of dazzling white linen showed him to be a man of decorous habits. His stained gloves might have been made for his small aristocratic hands, and when he took one off I was astonished to see the slenderness of his pale fingers. He had a casual, indolent walk, and I noticed that he did not swing his arms – a sure sign of secretiveness in a man. However, these are personal views based on my own observations and I have no wish to force them on other people.

When Pechorin sat down on the bench, his erect figure bent as though he hadn't a bone in his back. His whole posture gave the impression of some nervous debility. He sat in the manner of Balzac's thirty-year-old coquette[7] sitting in her cushioned armchair at the end of an exhausting ball. On first seeing his face I would have thought him no older than twenty-three, though later I would have taken him for thirty. There was something childlike in the way he smiled. His skin was delicate, like a woman's, and his naturally curly fair hair made a fine setting for the pale, noble brow. Only a prolonged scrutiny of his forehead revealed traces of criss-cross wrinkles that probably showed up much more in moments of anger or stress. Though his hair was fair, his moustache and eyebrows were black. In a man this is as sure a sign of breeding as a black mane and tail are in a white horse. I will finish my portrait by noting his slightly turned-up nose, brilliant white teeth and brown eyes.

I must say a little more about his eyes. In the first place, they never laughed when he laughed. Have you ever noticed this peculiarity some people have? It is either the sign of an evil nature or of a profound and lasting sorrow. His eyes shone beneath his half-lowered lids with a kind of phosphorescent brilliance (if one can put it like that). This brilliance was not the outward sign of an ardent spirit or a lively imagination. It was like the cold dazzling brilliance of smooth steel. When he looked at you, his quick, penetrating, sombre glance left you with the unpleasant feeling that you'd been asked an indiscreet question, and it would have seemed insolent had it not been so nonchalantly calm.

All these thoughts may have suggested themselves to me merely because I knew something of his life, and possibly he would have made an entirely different impression on someone else. Still, as you will hear nothing of Pechorin except from me, you must be content with the picture I give you. Let me conclude by saying that he was on the whole rather good-looking, with one of those unusual faces that appeal particularly to society women.

The horses were already harnessed. There was an occasional tinkle from the bell under the bow of the harness-frame. Twice Pechorin's servant came up to announce that all was ready, and still there was no sign of Maxim Maximych. Luckily, Pechorin was lost in thought, gazing at the jagged blue outline of the Caucasus, and seemed in no hurry to be off. I went up to him and said:

'If you'd care to wait a little longer you'll have the pleasure of meeting an old friend.'

'Ah, that's right,' he answered hastily. 'I was told about him yesterday. But where is he?'

I turned towards the square and saw Maxim Maximych running as fast as his legs could carry him. In a few minutes he was with us, gasping for breath, the sweat pouring from his face. Strands of wet grey hair sticking out from his cap clung to his brow. His knees were shaking. He was about to throw his arms round Pechorin, but Pechorin rather coldly held out his hand, although he gave him a friendly smile. For a moment the captain was too taken aback to do anything, but then eagerly grasped Pechorin's hand with both his own. He was still unable to speak.

'Delighted to see you, dear Maxim Maximych,' said Pechorin. 'How are you then?'

'And you, dear chap, . . . you, sir?' the old man mumbled, with tears in his eyes, put out by Pechorin's formal tone. 'It's been a long time . . . Where are you heading now?'

'Persia. Then on from there.'

'But you're not going this minute, are you? My dear fellow, you must stay on for a while. We're not going to part straight away after not seeing each other all this time.'

'It's time I left, Maxim Maximych,' replied Pechorin.

'But merciful heavens, man, what's all the rush? I've got so many things to tell you. So many things to ask as well. How is it then? Left the army, have you? What have you been doing?'

Pechorin smiled.

'Being bored,' he said.

'Do you remember the way we lived together at the fort? Grand hunting country that! You were a keen shot too, weren't you. And do you remember Bela?'

Pechorin paled slightly and turned away.

'Yes, I remember,' he said, and almost at once gave an affected yawn.

Maxim Maximych tried to persuade him to stay on for a couple of hours.

'We'll have a splendid dinner,' he said. 'I've got a couple of pheasants with me, and there's a fine Kakhetian wine here, not like you get in Georgia, of course, but first-class stuff . . . We'll have a talk. You can tell me what you've been doing in Petersburg. How about it?'

'My dear Maxim Maximych, I've really nothing to tell. Well, good-bye. I really must be off – I'm in a hurry.' He took his hand. 'Good of you to remember me.'

The old man frowned. He was grieved and cross, though he tried to hide it.

'Remember?' he growled. 'There's nothing wrong with *my* memory. Well, go your way then. I never thought we'd meet like this.'

Pechorin gave him a friendly hug.

'There now,' he said. 'I've not really changed, have I? But what can you do? We've all got our own way to go in life. Perhaps we'll meet again – who knows?'

As he said this he was already seated in the calash and the driver was gathering up the reins. Suddenly Maxim Maximych grabbed hold of the carriage door.

'Hey, wait a minute!' he shouted. 'I nearly forgot – I've got those papers you left behind. I've been carting them round with me. I thought I might come across you in Georgia, but now I've run into you here. So what shall I do with them?'

'Whatever you like,' said Pechorin. 'Good-bye.'

Maxim Maximych shouted after him:

'You're off to Persia then? When'll you be back?'

The carriage was already far away, but Pechorin gave a wave with his hand, as much as to say 'Probably never. What's there to come back for?'

Long after the jingle of the harness-bell and the rattle of the wheels over the stony road had faded poor old Maxim Maximych still stood there, deep in thought. At length, trying hard to look indifferent, despite the tears of vexation that glistened on his eyelashes, he said:

'We used to be friends, of course. But what's friendship these days? Why should he bother with me? I'm not rich or a high-up, am I? And anyway, we're no match in years. Did you see what a dandy he is now he's been back in Petersburg? How about that calash? And all that luggage, eh? And that stuck-up servant!'

He said this with an ironic smile. Then he turned to me.

'Tell me,' he said. 'What do you think? What's possessed him that he should want to go off to Persia? It's queer, it really is. I always knew he was flighty, of course, not the sort you can rely on. A pity he's got to come to a bad end, though. But it's bound to happen. As I've always said, no good ever comes of a man who forgets an old friend.'

He turned away to hide his feelings, then walked round his cart in the yard, pretending to inspect the wheels, while all the time there were tears welling in his eyes. I went up to him.

'Maxim Maximych,' I said. 'What are those papers Pechorin left you?'

'Heaven knows. Notes of some kind.'

'What are you going to do with them?'

'Me? Why, use them for cartridge wads, I suppose.'

'Why not give them to me instead?'

He looked at me in astonishment. Then growling some incoherent remark, he began rummaging through his valise. He pulled out a notebook and tossed it disdainfully on the ground. A second, a third were treated in similar fashion till there were ten in all. There was something childish in his being so cross. I was amused, yet felt sorry for him too.

'That's the lot,' he said. 'I wish you joy of them.'

'Can I do what I like with them?' I asked.

'Print them in the papers for all I care. It's no concern of mine. I'm not a friend of his am I, or a relation? True, we lived a good while under the same roof – but then I've lived with plenty of different people in my time.'

I snatched up the papers and carried them off in case the captain should regret his decision. Soon afterwards we were told the detachment would be leaving in an hour and I ordered the horses to be harnessed. I was already putting on my cap when Maxim Maximych came into the room. It seemed he was not getting ready to leave. There was an unnatural, cold air about him.

'What, aren't you going then?' I asked him.

'No.'

'Why ever not?'

'I've not seen the commandant yet, and I've got some government property to hand in.'

'But you've been to see him,' I said.

'Yes, I did go,' he stammered. 'He was out and . . . I didn't wait.'

I realized what he meant. Perhaps for the first time in his life the poor old fellow had neglected his duty 'in pursuit of personal ends' (as the official phrase goes) – and small thanks had he got for it.

'Maxim Maximych, I'm very sorry we're parting sooner than we'd thought,' I said.

'How can an uneducated old man like me keep up with you? You young society chaps, you're too stuck-up. As long as you're down here, with Circassian bullets flying round, you put up with fellows like me, but then you meet us afterwards and won't as much as offer your hand.'

'Maxim Maximych,' I said. 'I've done nothing to deserve these reproaches.'

'Oh, I was just speaking generally. No, I wish you luck and a pleasant journey.'

We said good-bye rather stiffly. Good kindly Maxim Maximych was now the pig-headed, crotchety captain. And the reason? All because Pechorin had without thinking, or for some other reason, offered his hand when Maxim Maximych had wanted to embrace him. It is sad to see a young man's fondest hopes and dreams shattered when the rose-coloured veil through which he has viewed the actions and feelings of men is plucked away. But still he has the hope of replacing his old illusions with others, just as fleeting, but also just as sweet. But what can replace them in a man of Maxim Maximych's age? Inevitably, he becomes crusty and withdrawn.

I left alone.

Pechorin's Journal

Foreword

Not long ago I heard that Pechorin had died on his way back from Persia. I was delighted, since it means that I can print his notes, and I readily take this opportunity of putting my own name to somebody else's work. I only hope the reader won't blame me for this innocent imposture.

I must now give some explanation of what prompted me to publish the innermost secrets of a man I never knew. It would have been different if I had been his friend, for we all know how treacherously indiscreet a true friend can be. But I only ever saw him once, and that in passing, so I cannot feel for him that inexpressible hatred which lurks beneath the mask of friendship and waits only for the death or downfall of the other in order to shower him with reproaches, advice, taunts and regrets.

Reading over these notes, I felt convinced of the sincerity of the man who so ruthlessly exposed his own failings and vices. The story of a man's soul, even the pettiest, can be more interesting and instructive than the story of a whole nation, especially if it is based on the self-observation of a mature mind and is written with no vain desire to arouse sympathy or surprise. The trouble with Rousseau's *Confessions*[1] is that he read them to his friends.

It is only from a wish to be of service that I am publishing these extracts from a journal which came into my possession by chance. I have changed all the names, but the people mentioned in it will probably recognize themselves. They may also find some excuse for things done by this man (now no longer of this world) for which they have until now censured him – we practically always excuse things when we understand them.

In this book I have included only the parts relating to Pechorin's time in the Caucasus; I have in my possession another thick notebook in which Pechorin recounts his whole life-story. Some day that too will be put before the public, but there are a number of important reasons why I cannot venture to undertake this at the moment.

Some readers might like to know my own opinion of Pechorin's character. My answer is given in the title of this book. 'Malicious irony!' they'll retort. I don't know.

I

Taman

Taman[1] is the foulest hole among all the sea-coast towns of Russia. I practically starved to death there, then on top of that someone tried to drown me. I arrived there late one night by stage. The driver pulled up the weary *troika* by the gate of the one stone house in the place, just at the entrance to the town. Hearing the harness-bell, a Black Sea Cossack[2] sentry gave a wild yell, half-asleep: 'Who goes there?' A Cossack sergeant and corporal came out. I explained I was an officer travelling on duty to my unit at the front and wanted a billet for the night. The corporal took us round the town. Every house we stopped at was full. It was cold, I'd had no sleep for three nights and was tired out. I began to lose my temper. 'Take me anywhere, you rogue!' I shouted. 'To the devil himself, as long as it's a place to sleep.' The corporal scratched the back of his head. 'There is one other place, sir, but you wouldn't fancy it. Unwholesome, it is.'

I didn't know what he meant by this last remark and told him to lead the way. We passed through a lot of filthy back-streets, seeing nothing but ramshackle fences, till finally we drove up to a small hut on the very edge of the sea.

A full moon shone on the thatched roof and white walls of my new abode. The yard had a rubble wall round it, and in the yard was another tumbledown shack, smaller and more ancient than the first. Almost at the foot of its walls there was a sheer drop to the sea, with dark blue waves splashing and murmuring unceasingly below. The moon looked calmly down on the turbulent element it ruled.

Some way off shore I could make out two ships in the moonlight, their black rigging motionless, silhouetted like a spider's web against the pale outline of the horizon. There are ships at the quay, so I can leave for Gelendzhik[3] tomorrow, I thought.

My batman was a Cossack from one of the frontier regiments. I told him to get my valise down and dismiss the driver, then called for the master of the house. There was no answer. I knocked, and still there was no answer. What did it mean?

In the end a boy of about fourteen crept out from the inner porch.

'Where's the master?' I asked.

'No master here,' answered the boy in Ukrainian.

'You mean there isn't a master at all?'

'That's right.'

'Well, where's the mistress?'

'Gone to the village.'

'Who'll open the door for me then?' I asked, giving it a kick. The door opened by itself, and a dank smell came from within. I lit a sulphur match and held it up to the boy's face. Its light showed a pair of wall-eyes: he was blind, totally blind from birth. He stood before me without moving, and I had a good look at his face.

I confess I'm strongly prejudiced against the blind, one-eyed, deaf, dumb, legless, armless, hunch-backed, and so on. I've noticed there's always some odd link between a person's outward appearance and his inner self, as though when a man loses a limb he loses some inner feeling as well.

So I studied the blind boy's face. But what can you expect to see in a face without eyes? I took a long look at him, and couldn't help feeling sorry for him, when suddenly the ghost of a smile flitted across his thin lips. For some reason this struck me very unpleasantly. I had an idea that this blind boy might not be so blind as he seemed. I told myself that there was no way of faking wall-eyes, and anyway why should he want to? But it was no good – prejudice often takes me this way.

In the end I said:

'You the son of the house?'

'No.'

'Who are you then?'

'A poor orphan.'

'Has the woman got any children?'

'No. She had a daughter, but she went off with a Tatar. Over the sea.'

'Who was this Tatar?'

'I don't know. A Crimean Tatar[4] he was, a boatman from Kerch.'

I went into the hut. There was no furniture apart from a table, a couple of benches and a huge chest by the stove. There wasn't a single icon[5] on the walls – a bad sign. The sea wind blew through a broken window-pane.

I took a stump of candle from my valise, lit it and unpacked. I stood my sabre and gun in the corner, laid my pistols on the table and spread my cape out on one of the benches, while my Cossack did the same on the other. Ten minutes later he was snoring, but I couldn't get to sleep. I kept seeing the wall-eyed boy before me in the darkness.

An hour or so passed. The moonlight shining through the window played on the mud floor of the hut. Suddenly a shadow flitted across the patch of moonlight on the floor. I sat up and looked at the window. Once more someone ran past it and vanished. I couldn't imagine that this person had run on down the vertical drop to the sea, but there was nowhere else he could have gone.

I got up, put on my *beshmet*, fastened my belt and dagger and crept silently out of the hut. Coming towards me was the blind boy. I hid by the fence and he walked past me, his step cautious, but sure. He had a bundle under his arm. Turning towards the quay, he started down the steep and narrow pathway. Then shall the dumb sing and the blind see,[6] I thought, and went after him, keeping close enough to have him in sight.

By now the moon was clouding over. A mist lay over the sea, and the stern lantern of the nearest ship glimmered faintly through it. Foaming breakers gleamed along the shore, threatening every minute to overwhelm it.

I made my way with difficulty down the steep slope and saw the blind boy pause at the bottom and turn right along the foot of the cliff. He walked very close to the water's edge and looked every moment as though he would be swept away by a wave. But judging by the sureness with which he jumped from rock to rock, avoiding the hollows, it was clearly not the first time he had taken this walk.

In the end he stopped and sat down on the beach, placing his bundle beside him and apparently listening for something. I watched his movements from behind a protruding rock. In a few minutes a white figure appeared from the other direction. It came up to the blind boy and sat down beside him. The wind brought me snatches of their conversation.

'What do you think, blind boy?' said a woman's voice. 'It's very rough. Yanko won't come.'

'Yanko's not afraid of storms,' said the blind boy.

'The mist's thickening,' said the woman, a note of sadness in her voice.

'It's easier to slip past the coastguards when it's misty,' replied the boy.

'And what if he's drowned?'

'What if he is? You'll go to church on Sunday without a new ribbon.'

There was silence. One thing had struck me, though – when the blind boy had talked to me he had spoken Ukrainian, but now he spoke pure Russian.[7]

'There, I was right,' said the blind boy, clapping his hands. 'Yanko's not afraid of sea or wind or mist or coastguards. Listen! That's not the sea splashing – it's Yanko's long oars. You can't fool me.'

The woman leapt up and peered anxiously out to sea.

'Rubbish,' she said. 'I can't see anything.'

I confess that, hard as I tried, I was unable to descry anything like a boat in the distance. Ten minutes went by, then, suddenly, a black speck appeared among the mountainous waves. One moment it grew bigger, the next smaller, rising slowly on the crests and dropping swiftly into the troughs of the waves. It was a boat coming in to shore. Bold was the sailor indeed who ventured to cross the fifteen miles of the straits on such a night, and pressing the reason for his doing so.

Turning this over in my mind, I watched with bated breath as the frail little craft dived like a duck into the abyss, then, beating its oars like wings, rose up again in a shower of spray. Next I thought it was going to be dashed to pieces on the shore, but it deftly turned broadside and slipped unscathed into the tiny bay.

Out of it stepped a man of middle height, wearing a Tatar sheepskin cap. He waved his hand and all three began lugging something out of the boat that was so heavy that I can't think why the boat hadn't sunk. They all took a bundle on their shoulders and set off along the shore. I soon lost sight of them. I had to get back, but I was very disturbed by these weird doings, I don't mind saying, and impatiently waited for morning to come.

When my Cossack woke up he was very surprised to find me fully dressed, but I didn't tell him the reason for it. I spent some time at the window admiring the view. The blue sky was dotted with scattered clouds, the far Crimean shore was a mauve streak on the horizon, ending in a cliff on top of which was the white tower of a lighthouse. I set out for the fort of Phanagoria[8] to find out from the commandant when I could leave for Gelendzhik. But, alas, the commandant couldn't give a definite answer. All the ships at the quay were either coastguard vessels or merchantmen that had still to take on cargo.

'There might be a packet boat in three or four days,' he said. 'We'll see about it then.'

I went back to my lodging, dejected and annoyed, to be met at the door by my Cossack, who looked scared.

'It looks bad, sir,' he said.

'Yes,' I answered. 'Heaven alone knows when we'll get out of here.'

At this he grew even more agitated and, leaning towards me, whispered:

'This place – it's unwholesome. I met up with a Black Sea Cossack I know today, a sergeant – he was in my unit a year back. When I told him where we were, he said the place was unwholesome and the people a bad lot. And he's right, too. What can you make of that blind boy? He goes everywhere on his own, fetches the water, goes down to the market for bread. Everybody here seems to take it for granted.'

'Well, what of it? Has the woman come back?'

'Yes, she came while you were out. She's brought her daughter.'

'Daughter? She hasn't got one.'

'Well, I don't know who she is if she's not her daughter. Anyway, the old woman's sitting there in the hut now.'

I went into the hovel. The stove was going full blast and the meal being cooked on it looked rather lavish for poor folk. All my questions to the old woman met with the reply that she was deaf and couldn't hear. There was no point in going on, so I turned to the blind boy, who sat in front of the stove, putting sticks on the fire. I took hold of his ear.

'Now then, you blind imp,' I said. 'Where were you going with that bundle last night, eh?'

The boy suddenly burst into tears, bawling and whining.

'Where to?' he said (once more in Ukrainian). 'I didn't go anywhere. Bundle? What bundle?'

This time the old woman heard.

'Making things up,' she grumbled, 'and blaming it on a poor afflicted boy. What are you getting on to him for? What's he done to you?'

I'd had enough of this and went out, determined to get to the bottom of this mystery.

Pulling my cape around me, I sat down on a stone by the fence and gazed into the distance. Before me lay the sea, still rough after last night's storm, and its monotonous din, like the murmur of a town as it falls asleep, reminded me of the old days and took my mind back to our cold northern capital. Stirred by these memories, I sat lost in thought.

An hour had gone by, perhaps more, when I suddenly heard what sounded like a song. Yes, it was a song, sung by the young, fresh voice of a woman. But where was it coming from? I listened. It was an odd tune, slow and melancholy, then quick and lively. I looked around, but there was nobody about. I listened again. The sound seemed to come from the sky. I looked up and there, standing on the roof of my hut, was a girl in a striped dress, with her hair flowing loose, a veritable mermaid. She was gazing out to sea, shielding her eyes from the sun with her hand. One moment she laughed, talking to herself, then she would take up her song again. I can remember every word of it.

> Tall ships sail o'er the deep green ocean,
> White sails set on the billowy wave.
> My little boat sails there with the tall ships,
> Sails has she none, just her two good oars.
> Storm winds will blow, and the old tall ships
> Will lift their wings and fly over the sea.
> Then I'll curtsey and beg so humbly:
> 'Have pity on my boat, oh wicked sea.
> 'Precious are the goods that my boat carries,
> 'Bold is the heart that steers her through the night.'

I couldn't help thinking that I'd heard this voice the night before. I thought for a moment, and when I next looked at the roof the girl was gone. Suddenly, she darted past me, humming a different tune and snapping her fingers, and ran inside to the old woman. There was an argument, the old woman speaking angrily, the girl laughing loudly. Then again I saw my undine[9] skipping towards me. She stopped as she reached me and stared me in the eye, as though surprised at my being there, then nonchalantly turned away and walked slowly off towards the quay.

That wasn't the end of it, though, because she was to and fro around my quarters all day, endlessly singing and skipping. She was a strange creature. There were no signs of madness in her face – in fact, when she looked at me, her eyes were bright and penetrating. They appeared to have some magnetic power and seemed always to be expecting some question, but as soon as I spoke, she would run off with a crafty smile.

I had never seen a woman like her before. She wasn't at all beautiful, though I have my prejudices on the subject of beauty too. She had plenty of breeding, and breeding in a woman, as in a horse, means a lot – a discovery first made by Young France.[10] It (breeding, that is, not Young France) comes out chiefly in a woman's walk, in her hands and feet, the nose being specially significant. In Russia a well-shaped nose is rarer than a tiny foot.

My singer appeared to be no older than eighteen. I was enchanted by the extraordinary suppleness of her figure, the special tilt she gave to her head, the golden tint of her lightly-tanned neck and shoulders, her long auburn hair, and, above all, her well-shaped nose. True, there was something wild and suspicious about her sidelong glances, and an elusive quality in the way she smiled, but such is the power of prejudice that my head was completely turned by her well-shaped nose. I thought I had lighted on Goethe's Mignon,[11] that fabulous product of his German imagination. Indeed, they had much in common – the same sudden changes of mood, from extreme unrest to complete inertia, the same enigmatic speeches, the same skipping, the same strange songs.

Late in the afternoon I stopped her in the doorway and we had the following conversation:

'Tell me, my pretty one,' I said. 'What were you doing up on the roof today?'

'Looking to see which way the wind blew.'

'And why did you want to know that?'

'Happiness comes the way the wind blows.'

'Was your song to bring you happiness then?'

'Happiness goes with a song.'

'And what if you sing yourself into trouble?'

'What if I do? If things don't get better, they get worse, and it's a short road that leads from bad to good.'

'Who taught you that song?'

'Nobody taught me. I sing whatever comes into my head. It'll be heard by who it's meant for, and who isn't meant to hear won't understand.'

'And what's your name, my songstress?'

'The man who christened me, he knows.'

'And who was he?'

'How should I know?'

'We are mysterious, aren't we,' I said. 'Well, there's something I do know about you.' There was no change in her expression, not even a flicker of her lips — I might have been talking of someone else. 'I know you went down to the shore last night.'

And I gave her a very solemn account of all that I had seen, expecting to confuse her, but not on your life! She just burst out laughing.

'It's plenty you saw, but little you know,' she said. 'And what you do know, keep it to yourself.'

'And supposing, for instance, I decided to report it to the commandant?' I said, looking extremely solemn, even severe.

With a sudden hop, however, she burst into song and vanished like a bird startled from a bush. My final words were inopportune. I had no idea of their importance at the time, but later had occasion to regret them.

As soon as it was dark, I told my Cossack to heat up the teapot camp-style, then lit a candle and sat down at the table, taking an occasional puff at my travelling pipe. I was just finishing my second glass of tea when the door creaked and I heard footsteps and the light rustle of a dress behind me. I gave a start and turned round. It was my undine. She quietly sat down opposite me, saying nothing, but gazing at me with a look that seemed wonderfully tender. It reminded me of those looks that had played such havoc with my life in the old days. She appeared to expect some question, but for some inexplicable reason I was overcome with embarrassment and said nothing. You could tell she was excited from the dull pallor of her face, and I noticed a faint tremor in her hand as it strayed aimlessly over the table. One moment her bosom heaved, the next she seemed to be holding her breath. I was beginning to feel I'd had enough of this comedy and was on the point of putting a highly prosaic end to the silence – by offering her a glass of tea – when she suddenly leapt up, threw her arms round my neck and a moist, passionate kiss sounded on my lips. It went black before my eyes, my head swam, and I embraced her with all the force of youthful passion. But, whispering in my ear 'Tonight when they're all asleep, come down to the shore', she slid snake-like through my arms and darted from the room. In the hallway she knocked over the teapot and the candle that stood on the floor.

'She-devil!' yelled my Cossack, who had settled down on some straw, intending to warm himself with what was left of the tea. Only then did I come down to earth.

Two hours later, when all was quiet on the quay, I roused my Cossack.

'If I fire my pistol, run down to the shore,' I said.

His eyes bulged, and he replied automatically, 'Very good, sir.' I stuck a pistol in my belt and went out.

She was waiting for me at the edge of the cliff. She was less than lightly dressed, with a flimsy shawl round her supple waist.

'This way,' she said. She took my hand and we began the descent. I still don't know how I escaped breaking my neck. At the bottom we turned to the right and took the path along which I had followed the blind boy the night before. The moon was not yet up, and two solitary stars shone like two warning lights in the deep blue sky. The ponderous waves came in with steady rhythmic beat, barely lifting the lone boat that lay moored by the shore.

'Let's get into the boat,' said my companion.

I hesitated. I'm not at all keen on sentimental boat-trips, but this was no time for holding back, so I followed her into the boat, and before I realized what was happening we were afloat.

'What's this all about?' I asked angrily.

'This is what it's about,' she said, pushing me on to the seat and putting her arms around my waist. 'I love you.'

Her cheek pressed against mine, and I felt her fiery breath upon my face. Suddenly there was a loud splash as something fell into the water. I grabbed for my belt – and found my pistol gone. I suddenly had a horrible suspicion. The blood surged in my head. I looked round – we were a hundred yards from shore and I couldn't swim! I tried to push her away, but she clung to my clothes like a cat, and with a sudden push nearly had me in the sea. The boat rocked, but I steadied myself, and a desperate struggle began. My fury gave me extra strength, but I saw I was no match for my opponent when it came to agility.

'What is it you want?' I cried, squeezing her tiny hands till the bones crunched. But with her serpentlike nature she bore the pain and made no cry.

'You saw,' she said. 'You'll tell on us.'

Then, with a superhuman effort, she hurled me across the gunwale, and we both hung half over the side of the boat, with her hair touching the water. It was a critical moment. Bracing my knee against the bottom of the boat, I seized the plait of her hair with one hand and her throat with the other. She let go of my clothes, and in an instant I pushed her into the sea. It was quite dark now. I glimpsed her head a couple of times in the spray, and that was all.

I found half an old oar in the bottom of the boat and after much labour somehow reached the quay. As I made my way back to the hut along the shore I automatically looked towards the place where the blind boy had awaited the nocturnal sailor the night before. The moon was now riding in the sky and I fancied I saw someone in white sitting on the beach. Filled with curiosity, I crept nearer and dropped down in the grass above the cliff. By raising my head slightly I had a good view of all that was going on below and was not very surprised, in fact I was almost glad, to see that it was my mermaid. She was wringing the spray from her long hair, and her wet frock showed the outline of her supple waist and high bosom.

A boat soon appeared in the distance. It came swiftly in to shore and a man got out, as on the previous night. He wore a Tatar cap, though his head was shaved like a Cossack, and he had a large knife sticking from his belt.

'Yanko,' said the girl. 'Everything's ruined.'

They went on talking, but so quietly that I couldn't catch what they were saying.

'Where's the blind boy?' asked Yanko at last in a louder voice.

'I've sent him for the things,' said the girl.

He appeared a few minutes later carrying a sack on his back, which was stowed in the boat.

'Listen you, blind boy,' said Yanko. 'Keep an eye on the place . . . you know where, don't you. There's valuable stuff there. Tell (I didn't catch the name) that I've finished taking orders from him. Things have gone wrong, and he won't see me again. It's too dangerous now. I'll go and look for a job somewhere else. He won't find another daredevil chap like me, and you tell him that Yanko would never have left him if he'd paid better. But I go where I please, wherever the wind blows and the sea roars.' There was a pause, then Yanko said: 'She's going with me. She can't stay here now. And tell the old woman it's time she died. She's lived too long, she's had her time. She won't see us again.'

'What about me?' asked the blind boy plaintively.

'You're no concern of mine,' said Yanko.

Meanwhile, my undine had jumped into the boat and waved to her companion. Yanko put something in the blind boy's hand and said:

'Here, buy yourself some gingerbread.'

'Is that all I get?' asked the blind boy.

'There's another then,' said Yanko, and I heard the ring of a coin falling on the rocks. The blind boy didn't pick it up.

Yanko got into the boat, and hoisting a small sail, they sailed swiftly away before the off-shore wind. For a long time the white sail could be seen in the moonlight, bobbing among the dark waves. The blind boy still sat on the shore, and I heard what sounded like sobbing. It was the boy crying. He cried and cried.

I felt sad. Why did fate toss me into the peaceful midst of these *honest smugglers*? Like a stone cast into a still pool I had shattered their calm – and like a stone, too, I had nearly gone to the bottom.

I went back to my lodging. The guttering candle flickered on a wooden platter in the hallway. Despite my orders, my Cossack was sleeping like a log, with his gun in his hands. I didn't disturb him, but took the candle and went inside the hut. To my dismay I found my box, silver-mounted sabre and Daghestan dagger (the gift of a friend) had all vanished. Now I knew what that damned boy had been carrying! I roused my Cossack with a none too friendly shove and cursed him angrily. But there was nothing I could do. It would have been absurd to go and complain to the authorities that I'd been robbed by a blind boy and very nearly drowned by a girl of eighteen.

Next morning there was a ship, thank God, and I left Taman. I've no idea what became of the old woman and the poor blind boy. And anyway, what are the joys and tribulations of mankind to me, an itinerant officer with a travel warrant in my pocket?

2

Princess Mary

11 May

I arrived in Pyatigorsk yesterday and took lodgings in the out-
skirts, high up at the foot of Mashuk.[1] When there's a storm the
clouds will come right down to my roof. When I opened my window
at five this morning, the room filled with the scent of flowers from
the modest garden outside. Branches of cherry blossom peep in at
my window and the wind sends occasional showers of white petals
on to my desk. I have magnificent views on three sides – to the west
lies Beshtau with its five blue peaks, like 'the last cloud of the dying
storm';[2] to the north Mashuk towers like a shaggy Persian cap,
filling the whole horizon; to the east the view is gayer – below me,
in a splash of colour, lies the little town, all neat and new, with the
babbling of medicinal springs and the clamour of the multi-lingual
throng. Beyond the town stands a massive amphitheatre of mountains, bluer and hazier in the distance, while along the horizon
stretches a silver chain of snowy peaks with Kazbek at one end and
the twin summits of Elbrus[3] at the other.

It's a delight to live in a place like this. Every fibre of my body
tingles with joy. The air is pure and fresh, as the kiss of a child,
the sun is bright, the sky is blue – what more can one want? What
need have we here of passions, desires, regrets?

However, enough of that. I'm off to the Elizabeth spring.[4] I
hear all the spa society gathers there in the morning.

*

I went down to the centre of the town and walked along the boulevard, meeting several pathetic groups going slowly up the hill. They were mostly steppe landowners' families, as you could tell at a glance from the husbands' old-fashioned threadbare coats and the dressy clothes of the wives and daughters. They evidently keep a check on all the young men of the spa, for they studied me with tender interest. They were taken in for a moment by the Petersburg cut of my coat, but when they saw my epaulettes were those of a mere line regiment, they indignantly turned away.

The wives of the local dignitaries – what you might call the ladies of the waters – were better disposed. They carry *lorgnettes* and bother less about a man's uniform, for, living in the Caucasus, they're used to finding ardent hearts and cultured minds under the plain numbered buttons and white cap of a line officer.[5] They are very charming ladies and their charm is not short-lived. They have a new set of admirers each year – perhaps that's the secret of their unfailing amiability.

As I climbed the narrow path to the Elizabeth spring, I passed a good number of men, some civilians, some soldiers, who, I later found out, form a special class among those awaiting the movement of the waters. They drink (though not the waters), rarely take walks, and are only half-heartedly interested in women. They spend their time gambling and complaining that they're bored. They are dandies, too, and strike classic poses as they lower their wicker-cased tumblers into the sulphur spring. The civilians sport pale blue cravats, and the military types have ruffs showing above their collars. They profess a profound scorn for all provincial houses and sigh for the aristocratic salons of the capital (where they are not received).

At last I came to the well. Just by it, on the little square, they have put up a red-roofed building to house the baths, and a short distance away there is a covered terrace where people can promenade when it rains. Some wounded officers were sitting on a bench, looking pale and sad, their crutches drawn in to their feet. A few ladies were walking briskly up and down the square, waiting for the waters to take effect. There were two or three pretty faces among them, and in the vine walks on the slopes of Mashuk I caught an occasional glimpse of the gaily-coloured bonnets of ladies fond of solitude *à deux* – for I saw that each bonnet was accompanied by a military cap or a monstrous round hat. Silhouetted on the steep cliff, where the pavilion called 'The Harp of Aeolus'[6] stands, were sightseers aiming their telescopes at Elbrus. Among them were two tutors and their charges, here to take the cure for scrofula.

I stopped, out of breath, at the edge of the cliff and leaned against the corner of the baths to look at the picturesque view all round. Suddenly I heard a familiar voice behind me.

'Why, Pechorin! Have you been here long?'

I turned round. It was Grushnitsky. We embraced. I'd first met him at the front. He'd been wounded in the leg and had come to the spa the week before me.

Grushnitsky is a cadet.[7] He's only been in the army a year and out of some peculiar brand of dandyism goes around in a thick private's greatcoat. He's got the soldier's St George's Cross.[8] He is well built, with dark complexion and black hair. To look at him you might take him for twenty-five, though in fact he is barely twenty-one. When he talks, he has a habit of tossing his head back, and all the time he twirls his moustache with his left hand, as he holds his crutch with his right. He speaks quickly, affectedly, and is one of those people who have a fine phrase ready for every occasion in life, but lack all sense of beauty and make a solemn display of uncommon emotions, exalted passions and exceptional sufferings. Their greatest pleasure in life is to create an effect, and romantic provincial ladies find them madly attractive. When they get older, they either settle down peaceably as country squires or take to drink, or occasionally both. There are often many good qualities in them, but never a scrap of poetry.

Grushnitsky has a special passion for declamation. The moment the conversation goes beyond ordinary topics he bombards you with words. I could never argue with him, for he never answers your objections or even listens to you. As soon as you stop speaking, he launches into a long tirade, supposedly bearing on what you said, but in fact merely continuing his own speech.

He is quite witty, and his epigrams are often amusing, though never pointed or savage – he'll never slay anyone with a word. He knows nothing of people or of the weaker sides of human nature, since the sole preoccupation of his life has been himself. His ambition is to become the hero of a novel. He's spent so much time trying to convince others that he's not of this world and that fate has some mysterious sufferings in store for him, that he practically believes it himself. That's why he flaunts the thick private's greatcoat.

I've seen through him, and that's why he dislikes me – though outwardly we are on the best of terms. He is reputed to be very brave, but I've seen him in action: he waves his sword and charges forward shouting, eyes half-closed. Not exactly the Russian type of bravery.

I don't like him either. I fancy one day our paths will cross and one of us will come off worst.

His being in the Caucasus is also due to his mania for romantic situations. I'm sure that he spent his last evening at home gloomily explaining to some pretty neighbour that he wasn't going just in the course of duty, but was going in search of death, because . . . At this point he no doubt hid his eyes and said 'No, you mustn't know the reason. The shock would be too great for your pure heart. Anyway, what point would there be? What am I to you? Will you ever understand me?' – and so on.

He told me himself that his reason for joining the K——regiment would for ever remain a secret between himself and the Almighty.

Still, when he drops the tragic line Grushnitsky is quite agreeable and entertaining. I'm curious to see him with women. I imagine he really puts it on then.

We met like old friends. I asked him about spa life and people of interest. He sighed.

'It's a pretty dull life we lead here,' he said. 'The people who drink water in the morning are lifeless like all invalids, and the ones who drink wine in the evening are insufferable like all healthy people. There's some female society – but that's small comfort. They play whist, dress badly and their French is terrible. There's only Princess Ligovskoy from Moscow this year. She's here with her daughter, but I'm not acquainted with them. My private's greatcoat stamps me as an outcast. I find it hard to take the sympathy it brings me – it's like charity.'

Just then two ladies walked past us towards the well, one elderly, the other young, with a good figure. I couldn't see the faces beneath their hats, but they were dressed in the strictest good taste – nothing excessive. The young one wore a high-necked pearl-grey dress, with a light silk scarf round her supple neck. Her dark brown boots fitted so trimly round her slender ankles that even a person uninitiated in the mysteries of beauty would have certainly gasped, if only with surprise. In her light, yet dignified walk there was a virginal quality too elusive to define, but obvious to the eye. As she passed us, there was a breath of that indescribable fragrance that sometimes wafts from the letter of a woman one loves.

'That's Princess Ligovskoy,' said Grushnitsky. 'And that's her daughter. She calls her Mary, in the English fashion. They've only been here three days.'

'Yet you know her Christian name already?'

Grushnitsky blushed.

'I happened to hear it,' he said. 'I must say I've no wish to make their acquaintance. These proud aristocrats think soldiers like us uncouth, because we're not in the Guards. Little they care what intellect or feeling there might be beneath a cap with just a number and a thick greatcoat.'

I smiled.

'Your poor greatcoat!' I said. 'And who's the man going up and giving them their glasses with such attention?'

'Oh, that's Rayevich, some dandy from Moscow. He's a gambler too – you can tell by the blue waistcoat and that enormous gold chain looped across it. Look how thick his stick is – it would do for Robinson Crusoe. So would the beard, for that matter, and his peasant's haircut.'

'You've got a down on the whole human race,' I said.

'I've good reason to.'

'Oh, really?'

At this point the ladies moved away from the well and came level with us. With the aid of his crutch Grushnitsky struck a dramatic pose and answered me loudly in French:

'*Mon cher, je haïs les hommes pour ne pas les mépriser, car autrement la vie serait une farce trop dégoutante.*'[9]

The pretty young princess turned and bestowed a long, curious look on the speech-maker. The feeling conveyed in her look was very hard to define, but it wasn't scorn – on which I felt Grushnitsky was to be warmly congratulated.

'This Princess Mary is very pretty,' I said. 'She's got such velvet eyes. "Velvet" is just the right word – I suggest you borrow it when you talk about her eyes. The top and bottom lashes are so long that the pupils don't reflect the sunlight. I like eyes that don't shine. They're so soft, they seem to stroke you. Actually, her whole face seems excellent. And are her teeth white? That's very important. Pity she didn't smile at that fine phrase of yours.'

'You talk about a pretty woman as if she were an English thoroughbred,' declared Grushnitsky indignantly.

'*Mon cher,*' I replied, trying to capture his tone. '*Je méprise les femmes pour ne pas les aimer, car autrement la vie serait un mélodrame trop ridicule.*'[10]

I turned and walked away. I spent half an hour strolling about the vine walks and limestone cliffs and the bushes on the slopes between. It was growing hot, so I hurried to get home.

As I passed the sulphur spring, I stopped to get my breath in the shade of the covered terrace and chanced to see a somewhat curious scene. The actors were placed as follows: the old princess and the Moscow dandy sat on a bench in the covered terrace, apparently deep in earnest talk; the young princess, having presumably finished her last glass of water, was walking pensively up and down near the well. Grushnitsky was standing by the well itself. There was no one else about.

I went closer and hid round the corner of the terrace. Just then Grushnitsky dropped his glass on the gravel and struggled to bend and pick it up, but was hampered by his wounded leg. Poor fellow, how hard he tried, leaning on his crutch, but all in vain. There was a look of quite genuine suffering on his expressive face. Princess Mary saw all this better than I did, and, light as a bird, she tripped forward, stooped, picked up the glass and gave it to him with a gesture of indescribable charm. Then she blushed deeply and looked back at the terrace, but once she had made sure that Mama had seen nothing, she immediately regained her composure. By the time Grushnitsky opened his mouth to thank her she was gone.

A minute later she came out of the terrace with her mother and Rayevich, but as she passed Grushnitsky she put on a look of solemn decorum and never turned or even noticed the long passionate look with which he followed her down the hill till she disappeared among the lime-trees on the boulevard. There was though a glimpse of her hat across the street as she stepped quickly through the gate of one of the best houses in Pyatigorsk. The old princess followed after taking leave of Rayevich at the gate.

Only then did the poor ardent cadet notice I was there.

'Did you see?' he said, shaking me firmly by the hand. 'She's an absolute angel.'

'Why?' I asked, looking all innocent.

'Do you mean you didn't see?'

'Certainly I saw. She picked up your glass. An attendant would have done the same if he'd been here, and a good deal quicker too, in hopes of a tip. Though it's easy enough to see why she felt sorry for you, after the terrible face you pulled when you put your weight on your shot leg.'

'And weren't you the least bit moved to see the way her face lit up?'

'No, I wasn't.'

I lied, but I wanted to bait him. I was born with a passion for contradiction. My whole life has been nothing but a series of dismal, unsuccessful attempts to go against heart or reason. An enthusiast turns me cold as ice, and I fancy that frequent contact with a languid phlegmatic would turn me into an ardent idealist. I admit, too, that at this moment I felt a twinge of something else, unpleasant, though familiar – envy. I say 'envy' straight out, for I'm accustomed to be frank with myself. And I doubt whether any young man, one, of course, who has lived in society and grown used to indulging his vanity, can avoid a pang of jealousy when he sees a pretty woman who's taken his idle fancy favour another, whom she knows no better than himself.

Grushnitsky and I went down the hill in silence, then walked along the boulevard. We passed the windows of the house into which our belle had vanished. She was sitting at the window. Grushnitsky tugged my arm and gave her one of those turbid, tender looks that have so little effect on women. I eyed her with my *lorgnette* and saw that she smiled at Grushnitsky's look, but was genuinely angered by my presumption. And, indeed, how dare a Caucasian line officer turn his *lorgnette* on a Moscow princess!

13 May

This morning the doctor called. His name is Werner, though he's a Russian.[11] There's nothing so odd about that – I once knew a man called Ivanov who was a German.

Werner is a remarkable man in many ways. Like most doctors, he's a sceptic and a materialist, but he's also a poet of the true sort – always a poet in what he does and often, too, in what he says, though he's never written a line of verse in his life. He's studied all the living chords of the human heart in the way other people might study the sinews of a dead body. He's never managed to apply his knowledge, though, just as a first-rate anatomist some-times has no idea how to cure a fever. As a rule Werner laughs at his patients behind their backs, but I once saw him in tears over a dying soldier. Werner was poor and dreamed of millions, but he would never lift a finger for the sake of money. He once told me he would rather do a favour to an enemy than a friend. The latter would mean selling his charity, while his enemy would hate him the more for his generosity.

He has a wicked tongue, and his epigrams have caused more than one good fellow to be written off as a common fool. His rivals, the jealous spa doctors, spread a rumour that he did caricatures of his patients. The patients were furious and most of them would have nothing more to do with him. His friends – every truly honest man serving in the Caucasus, that is – tried to restore his fallen stock, but failed.

He has one of those faces that seem disagreeable at first sight, but become attractive later, when one comes to recognize in its irregular features the mark of a tried and noble spirit. There have been cases of women falling madly in love with such people, preferring their ugliness to the beauty of the freshest, rosiest-cheeked Endymions.[12] Give women their due – they have an instinctive sense of inner beauty. Perhaps that is why men like Werner are so passionately fond of them.

Werner is short, thin and as weak as a child. He has one leg shorter than the other, like Byron, and his head looks dispro-portionately large for his body. His hair is close cropped, and shows up the bumps of his skull, which would astonish a phrenol-ogist by their strange mixture of opposing tendencies. His small black eyes are never still, always probing your thoughts. His dress is tasteful and neat, with his small, slender, sinewy hands resplendent in pale yellow gloves. His coat, cravat and waistcoat were invariably black. The young men always called him Mephis-topheles, and he pretended to be annoyed, though in fact it flattered his vanity.

We soon understood each other and became close acquaintances, for I'm incapable of friendship. Of two friends one is always the slave of the other, though often neither will admit it. I can never be a slave, and to command in these circumstances is too exacting, for you have to pretend at the same time. Besides, I have money and servants enough.

Our association began when I met Werner in S— at a noisy, crowded party of young men. As the evening wore on, the conversation turned to matters philosophical and metaphysical. They were discussing beliefs, and everyone believed in something or other.

'For my part,' said Werner, 'I'm convinced of only one thing.'

'What's that?' I asked, anxious to hear his views, for so far he had said nothing.

'That one fine day, sooner or later, I shall die,' he answered.

'I'm better off than you,' I said. 'I'm convinced of another thing too – that one foul evening I had the misfortune to be born.'

They all thought we were talking nonsense, though in fact no one had said anything more sensible than this the whole evening. From then on we marked each other out in the crowd, came together a number of times and discoursed very solemnly on abstract subjects until we saw that each of us was pulling the other's leg. Then we looked each other meaningly in the eye, as Cicero says the Roman augurs[13] did, and burst out laughing. We had a good laugh and separated, well pleased with our evening.

I was lying on the couch, gazing at the ceiling with my hands under my head, when Werner came into the room. He stood his cane in the corner, sat down, yawned and announced that it was getting hot outside. I said that I found the flies troublesome, and we both lapsed into silence.

'My dear Doctor,' I said. 'What a dull place the world would be if there were no fools. Here we are, two intelligent men, who know you can argue eternally about everything under the sun, so we don't argue. We each know practically all the other's innermost thoughts. With us a single word speaks volumes. We see through the triple outer husk to the kernel of our emotions. We find sad things funny and funny things sad, though in fact we're pretty indifferent to everything except ourselves. So there can be no exchange of feelings or ideas between us — we each know all we want to know about the other and have no wish to know more. All we can do is tell each other news. Have you got any to tell me?'

I closed my eyes and yawned, exhausted by this long speech.

Werner pondered a moment, then said:

'All that rigmarole of yours has got some purpose.'

'It's got two,' I replied.

'You tell me one, and I'll tell you the other,' he said.

'All right. You begin,' I said, still studying the ceiling, and smiling to myself.

'You'd like some information about a certain person who's arrived here. I can guess who it is you're interested in, because there have already been inquiries about you in that quarter.'

'Upon my word, Doctor, it's impossible for us to talk together. We read each other's minds.'

'And the other . . . ?'

'The other purpose was to make you talk — because firstly, listening is less exhausting than talking; secondly, there's no danger of saying more than you mean to; thirdly, there's the chance you might find out another's secret; and fourthly, an intelligent man like you prefers people who listen to people who talk. Now, to business. What did the old princess say about me?'

'You're quite sure it was the old princess and not the young one?'

'Absolutely.'

'Why?'

'Because the young princess asked about Grushnitsky.'

'You've a great gift of understanding,' said Werner. 'She told me she was sure the young man in the private's greatcoat had been reduced to the ranks because of a duel.'

'I trust you left her with that pleasant illusion?'

'Naturally.'

PARADOX

'The stage is set,' I cried, delighted. 'We'll see if we can provide a *dénouement* for this comedy. Evidently fate means to see I'm not bored.'

'I fancy poor Grushnitsky's going to be your victim.'

'Go on with your story, Doctor.'

'The old princess said your face seemed familiar. I said she must have met you in Petersburg. She knew your name when I mentioned it. Your affair seems to have caused quite a stir.[14] The princess talked about your escapades – society gossip with something of her own thrown in, I dare say. The daughter was very interested and evidently saw you as the hero of some novel in the modern taste. I didn't contradict the princess, though I knew she was talking nonsense.'

'You're a friend indeed,' I said and held out my hand. Werner shook it warmly.

'I'll introduce you if you like,' he said.

'Really, Doctor,' I said, throwing up my hands in horror. 'Heroes are never introduced. There's only one way for them to meet the girl, and that's to save her from certain death.'

'Are you really going to court the young princess then?'

'No, no, quite the contrary. I triumph at last, Doctor – you fail to understand me.' I paused for a moment. 'And yet I'm sorry you do,' I went on. 'I never give away my secrets, I greatly like people to guess them, since that way I can always disown them when it suits me. However, you must give me a description of the mother and daughter. What are they like?'

'The mother, for a start, is a woman of forty-five. She's got a splendid digestion, but there's something wrong with her blood – she's got red patches on her cheeks. She's spent the latter half of her life in Moscow and has put on weight with the quiet life she's led there. She's fond of spicy stories and she's sometimes vulgar in what she says herself when the daughter's not there. She told me her daughter's as pure as a dove. What do I care? I felt like telling her not to worry, as I wouldn't tell anyone. The mother's taking the cure for rheumatism, and the daughter for God knows what. I told them both to take two glasses of sulphur water a day and tempered baths twice a week. The old princess doesn't seem used to giving orders, and has got a great respect for her daughter's intelligence and learning because she's read Byron in English and knows algebra. The girls in Moscow seem to have gone academic. Good for them! The men are such boors anyway that flirting with them must be more than any intelligent woman can stand. The old princess has a great liking for the young men, but the daughter regards them with some scorn. She's picked that up in Moscow, where middle-aged wits are the staple fare.'

'Have you ever been in Moscow, Doctor?'

'Yes, I had something of a practice there once.'

'Do go on.'

'I think I've told you everything. Oh no, there's one more thing. The young princess seems to like talking about emotions, passions and that sort of thing. She's had one winter in Petersburg and didn't like it, especially the society life. She probably had a cool reception.'

'You saw no one at their house today?'

'Yes, I did. There was an adjutant, an affected Guards officer and a lady, who is newly arrived here. She's related to the princess by marriage. Very pretty, but very ill by the look of things. You may have met her at the well? Average height, fair hair, regular features, looks consumptive from the colour of her face. She's got a dark mole on her right cheek. I was struck by her – she's got a very expressive face.'

'A mole,' I muttered. 'Is it possible?'

Werner looked at me, put his hand on my heart and declared triumphantly:

'You know her!'

It was true, my heart was beating faster than normal.

'It's your turn to crow,' I said. 'But I trust you won't give me away. Though I've not yet seen her, I'm sure from your description that it's a woman I once loved long ago. Don't say a word to her about me. If she asks, say something bad about me.'

'As you please,' said Werner, with a shrug.

When he'd gone, I felt a desperate pang of sadness. Had Fate again brought us together here in the Caucasus? Or had she come on purpose, knowing she would meet me? How would we meet? And, anyway, was it her? My premonitions have never deceived me. There's no one so susceptible to the power of the past as I am. Every memory of past joy or sorrow stabs at my heart and strikes the same old chords. It's silly the way I'm made: I forget nothing – absolutely nothing.

After dinner, at about six o'clock, I walked along the boulevard. There were a lot of people. Princess Ligovskoy and her daughter were sitting on a bench, surrounded by young men all doing their utmost to make themselves agreeable. I positioned myself on another bench some distance away and stopped two officers I knew from the D— regiment. I began spinning some tale, and it must have been very funny, for they roared with laughter. Some of the princess's entourage came over to see what was up, and gradually they all drifted away to join my group. I kept on talking. My stories were clever to the point of stupidity, my comments on the oddities of the passers-by biting to the point of fury. I kept my audience amused till sunset. Princess Mary walked past several times on her mother's arm, escorted by an old fellow with a limp, and several times, as her eye fell on me, she looked annoyed, despite her efforts to appear indifferent.

'What was he telling you?' she asked one young man who, out of politeness, had gone back to her. 'It must have been most interesting. Perhaps it was about his exploits in battle?'

She said this quite loudly, most likely intending to pique me.

'Aha!' I thought. 'You're really angry, my dear Princess. Just wait. There's more to come.'

Grushnitsky followed her around like some predatory animal, never taking his eyes off her. I bet tomorrow he'll be asking for someone to introduce him to the mother. She's bored, so she'll be very pleased.

16 May

My affairs have come on tremendously these last two days. Princess Mary positively hates me. I've already heard two or three epigrams she has made up about me, quite pointed, but very flattering all the same. She just can't understand why I, who am used to good society and on such close terms with her Petersburg cousins and aunts, don't attempt to make her acquaintance. We meet every day at the well or on the boulevard, and I try my best to draw away her admirers – the glittering adjutants, the pale Muscovites, and so on – and I almost always succeed. I've always hated entertaining, but now every day my house is full of guests, dining, supping, gambling. It's a sad fact, but my champagne is more than a match for her magnetic eyes.

I met her in Chelakhov's shop[15] yesterday. She was haggling over the price of a splendid Persian rug and pleading with Mama not to begrudge her it, as it would look so nice in her study. I offered forty roubles more and bought it from under her nose. I was rewarded with a ravishing look of fury. Near dinner time I had my Circassian horse walked specially past her windows with the rug draped over him. Werner was visiting them at the time and told me that the effect of this scene was most dramatic. Princess Mary wants to launch a crusade against me, and I've noticed that two of the adjutants bow very stiffly to me when they are with her – but every day they dine at my table.

Grushnitsky has put on a militant air. He goes around with his hands behind his back, recognizing no one. His leg has suddenly got better, and he hardly limps at all. He's found some opportunity of talking to Princess Ligovskoy and paying some compliment to Princess Mary. She can't be very discriminating, for since then she's been responding with the sweetest smile when he bows to her.

'Are you quite sure you don't want to meet the Ligovskoys?' he asked me yesterday.

'Quite sure,' I said.

'But really! It's the most agreeable house in the place. All the best people . . .'

'My dear fellow, I've had enough of society anywhere, let alone this place. Do you visit them then?'

'Not as yet. I've talked a couple of times with the daughter, that's all. But it's rather embarrassing angling for an invitation, even if it is the done thing here. It'd be a different matter if I were commissioned.'

'Oh, come now. You're far more interesting as you are. You just don't know how to make the most of your advantages. Why, with that private's greatcoat, every sentimental girl takes you for a hero, a martyr.'[16]

Grushnitsky smiled conceitedly.

'Nonsense,' he said.

'I'm sure the daughter is in love with you already,' I went on.

He blushed violently and puffed himself up.

Oh, vanity! You are the lever with which Archimedes wanted to lift the world.

'You're always joking,' he said, pretending to be angry. 'In the first place, she scarcely knows me as yet.'

'Women only love men they don't know.'

'Naturally, I'm not in the least concerned that she should like me. All I want is to make the acquaintance of a pleasant family. It would be absurd for me to have any hopes . . . Now, with you, for example, it's another matter. A single look from one of you Petersburg lady-killers and women melt. Do you know what Princess Mary said about you?'

'What, she's been talking to you about me already?'

'It's nothing to be pleased about, I'm afraid. I happened to get into conversation with her at the well and practically the first thing she said was "Who is that disagreeable, sombre-looking man? He was with you the other day, when . . ." And she blushed. She wouldn't say which day, when she remembered the charming thing she had done. I told her there was no need to mention the day as it would live in my memory for ever. Pechorin, my friend,

I'm afraid you're in her bad books. It's such a pity, for Mary is awfully sweet.'

I should point out that Grushnitsky is one of those men who refer to any woman they scarcely know as 'my Mary', 'my Sophie', if she has the good fortune to appeal to him.

I looked serious, then said:

'Yes, she's not bad looking. But take care, Grushnitsky. Most Russian girls usually only go in for Platonic attachments with never a thought of marriage. And Platonic love is the most troublesome sort. The princess, I fancy, is one of those women who want to be amused, and two dull minutes with you will finish you for good. Your silence must rouse her curiosity, your conversation must leave her wanting more. You've got to play on her feelings all the time. She'll scorn public opinion a dozen times for your sake and call it a sacrifice, but she'll get her own back by tormenting you, and then later simply declare that she can't stand you. If you don't get the upper hand, her first kiss won't give you the right to expect a second. She'll play with you till she's tired of it, then a couple of years later she'll marry some brute out of duty to Mama and persuade herself she's unhappy, because it was not heaven's will to unite her with the only man she ever loved (you, that is) on account of his private's greatcoat, though under that thick grey coat there beat an ardent, noble heart . . .'

Grushnitsky banged his fist on the table and began pacing the room.

I laughed inwardly, and even smiled a couple of times, though luckily he didn't see me. He's more confiding than ever, so he must be in love. He's even come out with a silver niello ring made by a local craftsman. I thought it looked fishy, so I examined it, and what did I find? It's got the name 'Mary' engraved in small letters on the inside and next to it the date when she picked up the celebrated glass. I kept my discovery to myself. I don't want to force confessions from him, I want him to pick me as his confidant – then I'll have fun!

*

I got up late today, and when I got to the well, there was no one there. It was getting hot. Small fluffy white clouds were racing in from the snowy mountains, giving promise of a storm. The summit of Mashuk smoked like an extinguished torch, and wisps of grey cloud coiled and slid round it like snakes, as though entangled and held back in their course by the thorny scrub. The air was vibrant with electricity.

I went into the vine walk that leads to the grotto.[17] I felt sad, thinking of the young woman with the mole on her cheek that Werner had told me about. Why was she here? And was it her? And why did I think it was her? Why was I even sure of it? There are plenty of women with moles on their cheeks.

It was with these thoughts going through my mind that I came to the grotto. A woman was sitting on a stone seat in the cool shade of its vault. She wore a straw hat and was wrapped in a black shawl. Her head was sunk on her breast, her face hidden by her hat. Not wishing to disturb her meditation, I was about to turn back, when she glanced up at me.

'Vera!' I cried involuntarily.

She gave a start and turned pale.

'I knew you were here,' she said.

I sat beside her and took her hand. A long-forgotten thrill passed through my body at the sound of that sweet voice. Her deep, tranquil eyes looked straight into mine, and there was mistrust and something like reproach in them.

'It's been a long time,' I said.

'Yes, it's been a long time. We've both changed a lot.'

'You no longer love me, then?' I said.

'I'm married,' she said.

'Again? But it was the same a few years back, and then it didn't . . .'

She snatched her hand from mine, her cheeks blazing.

'Perhaps you love your second husband?'

She made no reply and turned away.

'Or is he very jealous?'

Silence.

'What then? He must be young, handsome, very rich (that's certain), and you're afraid . . .'

I looked at her and was alarmed by the look of utter despair on her face and the tears gleaming in her eyes.

At last she said in a whisper:

'Tell me, does it amuse you very much to torture me? I ought to hate you. Ever since I've known you, you've brought me nothing but suffering . . .'

Her voice trembled, she leaned towards me and lowered her head upon my breast.

Perhaps that's why you loved me, I thought. Moments of happiness one forgets, but sorrow never.

I clasped her tight in my arms, and so we stayed for a long time, till in the end our lips came close and met in a thrilling, passionate kiss. Her hands were like ice, her head was burning. And then we had one of those conversations which make no sense on paper, which you can't repeat and can't even remember. The meaning of the sounds supplants and enhances the meaning of the words, like in an Italian opera.

She is most anxious I shouldn't meet her husband. He is the old fellow with the limp I saw on the boulevard. She married him for the sake of her son. He's rich and suffers from rheumatism. I didn't allow myself a single gibe at his expense, for she respects him like a father – and will deceive him like a husband. The human heart is a funny thing, particularly the heart of a woman.

Vera's husband, Sergei Vasilievich G—v, is distantly related to Princess Ligovskoy. They live next door to her, and Vera often visits them. I promised Vera I would get an introduction to the Ligovskoys and show an interest in the daughter so as to divert attention from her. This doesn't in the least interfere with my plans. I shall enjoy myself.

Enjoy myself! I've passed that stage in life when all one seeks is happiness and when the heart feels the need to love someone with passion and intensity. Now all I want is to be loved, and by very few people at that. I think I'd even be content with just one lasting attachment – such is the heart's pathetic way.

It's always puzzled me that I've never been a slave to the women I've loved. In fact, I've always mastered them, heart and soul, without even trying. Why is it? Is it because I never care deeply for anything, while they have gone in constant fear of losing me? Or is it the magnetic attraction of a strong personality? Or have I simply never met a woman of real spirit?

I must confess I don't really like strong-willed women. That's not their role in life!

Actually, I do recall one occasion when I loved a woman with a will too strong for me to master. We parted enemies, though perhaps if I'd met her five years later we would have parted differently.

Vera is ill, very ill, though she won't admit it. I'm afraid it might be consumption or what they call *fièvre lente*,[18] a foreign ailment that has no name in Russian.

The storm broke while we were in the grotto and delayed us half an hour. She never asked me to swear to be true or to say if I'd loved other women since we had parted. She trusts me now as unthinkingly as before, and I won't deceive her. She is the one woman in the world I could never deceive. I know we shall soon part again, perhaps this time for ever. We shall each take our own road to the grave, but her memory will ever be sacred in my heart. I've told her this always and she believes me, though she says she doesn't.

At last we parted. I watched her go, till I lost sight of her hat among the rocks and shrubs. I felt a pang in my heart, as I did at our first parting. How I rejoiced to feel it. Was it youth coming back to me with all its healthy passions, or was it just youth's farewell glance, a parting gift to remember it by? It's absurd when you think that I'm still just a boy to look at. My face is fresh for all its paleness; my limbs are slim and supple; my hair is thick and curly; there's light in my eyes and fire in my blood.

When I reached home, I got on my horse and galloped out

into the steppe. I love galloping through long grass on a fiery horse, with the wind of the wilds in my face. I gulp the scented air and peer into the blue distance, trying to make out the hazy shapes that show up more distinctly every minute. Whatever sorrow weighs on the heart, whatever anxiety troubles the mind, it vanishes in a moment. You feel peace at heart, and the troubled mind is cleared by bodily fatigue. There's no woman whose eyes I wouldn't forget when I see the blue sky and the wooded mountains, lit by the southern sun, or hear the roar of a cascading torrent.

I fancy the Cossacks gazing idly from their watch-towers must have puzzled long over the sight of me galloping without cause or purpose, for from my clothes they must have taken me for a Circassian. Actually, I've been told that on horseback and in Circassian dress I look more like a Kabardian than many Kabardians themselves. Indeed, when it comes to this noble warrior's dress, I'm quite a dandy: just the right amount of braid, expensive weapons with a plain finish, the fur on my cap neither too long nor too short, close-fitting leggings and boots, a white *beshmet* and a dark maroon top-coat. I've made a long study of how the hillmen sit a horse, and nothing flatters my vanity more than to be admired for my mastery of the Caucasian riding style. I keep four horses, one for myself and three for my friends, to avoid the tedium of roaming the countryside on my own. They're pleased to take my horses, but never ride with me.

It was not till six o'clock that I remembered it was time for dinner. My horse was dead-beat. I came out on the road that leads from Pyatigorsk to the German colony,[19] where people from the spa often go *en pique-nique*.[20] The road winds through patches of scrub and drops into small ravines where roaring streams flow in the shade of tall grass; all round, like an amphitheatre, soar the massive blue mountains – Beshtau, Zmeinaya, Zheleznaya, Lysaya.[21]

In one of these ravines (called locally *balki*) I stopped to water my horse. Just then a glittering, noisy cavalcade came into view along the road, ladies in black or blue riding habits, their escorts in an incongruous mixture of Circassian and Russian costume. At the head rode Grushnitsky and Princess Mary.

Ladies at the spa still believe that the Circassians attack people in broad daylight, and probably because of this Grushnitsky had slung a sabre and a pair of pistols over his private's greatcoat. He looked quite absurd in this heroic attire.

I was hidden by a tall bush, but had a good view of everything through the foliage, and could tell from their faces that they were having a sentimental conversation. They came to the slope, and Grushnitsky took Princess Mary's horse by the bridle. I heard the tail-end of their conversation.

'And are you going to spend the rest of your life in the Caucasus?' asked the princess.

'What is Russia to me?' replied Grushnitsky. 'A country where thousands will scorn me because they are richer than I am, while here my thick greatcoat has not stood in the way of my meeting you.'

The princess blushed.

'Quite the reverse,' she said.

Grushnitsky looked pleased and went on:

'My life will pass stormily, swiftly and unnoticed among the bullets of savage tribesmen, and if each year God grants me one woman's glance as radiant as . . .'

At this point they drew level with me, and, whipping my horse, I rode out from behind the bush.

'*Mon dieu, un circassien!*'[22] cried the princess in horror.

To reassure her completely, I made a slight bow and replied in French:

'*Ne craignez rien, madame. Je ne suis pas plus dangereux que votre cavalier.*'[23]

She was covered with confusion. Was it because of her mistake? Or was it because she thought my reply insolent? I'd rather the latter were correct. Grushnitsky gave me a look of displeasure.

Late in the evening, about eleven, I went for a stroll through the lime walk on the boulevard. The town was asleep, and only in a few windows were there lights. On three sides there were black mountain ridges, offshoots of Mashuk, on whose summit a small, ominous cloud rested. The moon was rising in the east, and in the distance gleamed the silver fringe of snow-capped mountains. The cries of the sentries merged with the roar of the hot springs which are left to run freely during the night. Occasionally a clatter of hoofs rang along the street, accompanied by the creak of a Nogai's[24] cart and a doleful Tatar song.

I sat on a bench and pondered. I felt the need to talk to some friend, to pour out my thoughts to somebody. But to whom could I do that? I wondered what Vera was doing at that moment. I'd have given a lot to press her hand just then.

Suddenly I heard footsteps, quick and uneven. It sounded like Grushnitsky, and so it was. I asked him where he had been.

'At Princess Ligovskoy's,' he answered very grandly. 'How well Mary sings!'

'Do you know what?' I said. 'I bet she's no idea you're a cadet and thinks you're an officer who's been reduced to the ranks.'

'She might. What do I care?' he replied absently.

'I just mentioned it,' I said.

'You know, she's furious with you about today. She thought it was a terrible cheek, and I had a job to convince her that you couldn't have meant to offend her, being so well educated and knowing society as you do. She says you look insolent and must think very highly of yourself.'

'She's perfectly right. Aren't you going to take her part then?'

'I'm afraid I haven't the right as yet.'

Aha! I thought, you've got hopes then!

'But it's worse for you,' said Grushnitsky. 'You won't find it easy to get an introduction now. Such a pity. It's quite one of the most agreeable houses I know.'

I smiled to myself.

'The most agreeable house for me at the moment is my own,' I said, yawning, and got up to go.

'Still, why not admit you regret it?' said Grushnitsky.

'Nonsense! If I feel like it, I'll call on the princess tomorrow evening.'

'We'll see about that!'

'I'll even make advances to Princess Mary if you'd like me to.'

'Oh, yes! – supposing she'll speak to you.'

'I'll just wait till she's fed up with listening to you. Good night.'

'I'm going for a stroll,' said Grushnitsky. 'I just couldn't sleep at the moment. I know – let's go to the restaurant. There'll be gambling, and tonight I must have strong sensations.'

'I hope you lose,' I said, and went home.

21 May

Nearly a week has gone by and I still haven't met the Ligovskoys. I'm waiting for an opening. Grushnitsky follows Princess Mary everywhere like a shadow, and they have endless talks. When will she tire of him? Her mother takes no notice of them, since Grushnitsky is 'not eligible'. Such is the logic of mothers! I've noticed two or three tender looks being exchanged – I must put an end to it.

Yesterday Vera was at the well for the first time. She hasn't been out since we met in the grotto. We lowered our glasses into the well together and, as she leaned over, she whispered:

'Aren't you going to get an introduction to the Ligovskoys then? It's the only place we can meet.'

A reproach. How tedious! Still, I'd earned it.

Incidentally – tomorrow there's a subscription ball in the restaurant saloon, and I'm going to dance the mazurka with Princess Mary.

22 May

The hall of the restaurant had transformed itself into the hall of the Assembly Rooms. By nine o'clock everyone was there, the princess and her daughter among the last to arrive. Many ladies eyed her with envy and malice, because Princess Mary knows how to dress. Those who consider themselves the local aristocracy hid their envy and attached themselves to her. What can you do? In any female society you always get an upper and a lower circle.

Grushnitsky stood in the crowd beneath the window, pressing his face to the glass and never taking his eyes off his goddess. She gave him the slightest nod as she passed, and he beamed all over his face.

The dancing began with a *polonaise*, then a waltz was struck up and spurs jingled, coat-tails flew and whirled.

I stood behind a fat lady canopied with pink feathers. The splendour of her dress recalled the age of farthingales,[25] and the mottled colour of her coarse skin the happy days of the beauty spot. The biggest wart on her neck was concealed by a clasp. She was talking to her partner, a captain of dragoons.

'That young Princess Ligovskoy is quite insufferable,' she said. 'Think of it – she bumped against me and never even apologized, and then turned round and quizzed me with her glass. *C'est impayable!*[26] Why should she be so high and mighty? She needs to be taught a lesson.'

'That shouldn't be difficult,' replied the obliging captain, and he went off into the next room.

I at once went up to Princess Mary and asked if she would waltz, taking advantage of the free and easy ways of the place which allow you to dance with ladies you're not acquainted with.

She could scarcely suppress a smile and conceal her triumph, but soon managed to assume an air of complete indifference, even severity. She casually rested her hand on my shoulder, gave a slight tilt to her head, and we took the floor. I've never known a waist more sensuous or supple. The freshness of her breath was on my face, and occasionally a lock of her hair detached itself in the whirl of the dance and brushed against my burning cheek.

We did three turns (she waltzes amazingly well), at the end of which she was panting, with misted eyes and half-open lips that could barely murmur the obligatory '*Merci, monsieur*'.

For a few minutes neither of us spoke. Then, looking very humble, I said:

'Princess, I've heard that, though we're not acquainted, I've had the misfortune to earn your displeasure, and that you've found me impertinent. Can this be true?'

'And now you want to confirm me in my opinion?' she replied with an ironic look that actually goes very well with her mobile features.

'If I've had the effrontery to offend you in any way, then please permit me to have the even greater effrontery to ask your pardon. Really, I should very much like to prove that you were wrong about me.'

'You'd find that rather difficult,' she said.

'Why is that?'

'Because you don't call on us, and these balls are unlikely to be very frequent.'

So their doors are shut to me for ever, I thought.

'You know, Princess,' I said, with some annoyance. 'You should never reject a penitent transgressor. Despair might make him twice as bad as he was before, and then . . .'

Guffaws and whispers near by made me break off and look round. A few steps away there was a group of men, among them the dragoon captain who had declared hostile intentions against the charming princess. He was looking very pleased about something, rubbing his hands and laughing and winking at the others. Then a red-faced fellow with long whiskers wearing a tail-coat detached himself from the group and unsteadily walked straight towards

Princess Mary. He was drunk. He stopped in front of the embarrassed princess, put his hands behind his back and fixed her with his dull grey eyes.

'*Permettez* . . .' he began in a cracked falsetto. 'Oh, hang it all – look here, I'm booking you for the mazurka . . .'

'What is it you want?' she asked, her voice trembling. She looked round beseechingly, but unfortunately her mother was nowhere near and none of the men she knew were at hand. One of her adjutant friends, I fancy, did see what was happening, but hid in the crowd to avoid being involved in a scene.

'Well, what about it?' asked the drunk, with a wink to the dragoon captain, who was making signs to egg him on. 'Do you mean you don't want to? Then again I have the honour . . . to ask you *pour mazure* . . . Maybe you think I'm drunk? Doesn't matter! Improves my dancing, believe me . . .'

I could see she was on the point of fainting from terror and indignation. I went up to the drunk fellow, gripped him firmly by the arm, looked him hard in the face, and asked him to leave, since, I said, the princess had long promised to dance the mazurka with me.

'Too bad . . . Some other time,' he said, laughing, and went off to his abashed companions, who at once led him away into the next room.

I was rewarded with a marvellous, heart-felt look.

The princess went up to her mother and told her all about it, and the old princess sought me out in the crowd to thank me. She told me she knew my mother and was on friendly terms with half a dozen of my aunts.

'I can't think how it is we've not met before,' she added. 'But you must admit that it's all your fault. You're so aloof, I've never known anything like it. I hope your spleen will be dispelled by the atmosphere of my drawing-room. Do you think it might?'

I replied with one of those stock phrases which everyone must have ready for such occasions.

The quadrilles went on for ages, but at last the orchestra struck up the mazurka, and Princess Mary and I sat down.

I made no allusion to the drunk, or to my previous behaviour or Grushnitsky. She gradually got over the effects of the unpleasant scene, and her face brightened up. She bantered charmingly and talked in a lively, natural, unpretentiously witty way. Some of her remarks were quite profound. In a muddled sentence I let her know that I had long been attracted to her. She inclined her head and blushed slightly. Then she looked up at me with her velvet eyes and said, with a forced laugh:

'You're a strange man.'

'I didn't want to be introduced to you,' I went on, 'because you have so many admirers I was afraid of being lost in the crowd.'

'You needn't have feared that. They're all exceedingly dull.'

'What, all of them? Do you really mean that?'

She looked at me closely, as though trying to recall something, then again blushed slightly and said emphatically:

'Yes, every one.'

'Even my friend Grushnitsky?' I asked.

'Oh, is he a friend of yours?' she said, with some show of doubt.

'Yes, he is.'

'Well, naturally, I wouldn't class him as dull . . .'

'But you would class him as unfortunate!' I laughed.

'Certainly. Do you find that amusing? I wish you were in his place.'

'What's wrong with it? I was a cadet myself once, and I think it was the best time of my life.'

'Is he a cadet then?' she asked hastily. 'I always thought . . .'

'What?'

'Oh, nothing. Who is that lady?'

The conversation took another direction and the subject was dropped.

The mazurka ended and we parted – until our next meeting.

The ladies went home. As I went off to supper, I bumped into Werner.

'Aha!' he said. 'So much for you! The man who wasn't going to meet the princess except by saving her from certain death!'

'I did better,' I said. 'I saved her from fainting at a ball.'

'What happened? Tell me about it.'

'No. You're such a master of guesswork, fathom it out for yourself.'

23 May

I was walking on the boulevard at about seven o'clock, when Grushnitsky spotted me in the distance and came over. His eyes were shining with an absurd look of rapture. He shook me warmly by the hand and said in a tragic voice:

'Pechorin, my thanks! You know what I mean?'

'No, I don't. But whatever it is, don't bother to thank me,' I said, not having any good deed on my conscience.

'What? But what about yesterday? You can't have forgotten. Mary has told me everything.'

'Do you share everything with her now, then? Even gratitude?'

'Look,' he said, very dignified. 'If you wish to remain my friend, kindly refrain from making fun of my love. Do you understand, I love her madly . . . and I think, I hope, she loves me too. I want to ask you a favour. You'll be visiting them this evening – will you promise to take note of all she does? I know you're more experienced in these matters and know more about women than I do. Women! Women! Who can understand them? Their smile says one thing, their eyes another, their words lead you on with promises, but their tone of voice repulses you. One moment they guess your innermost thoughts, and the next they can't understand the most obvious hints. Take the princess, for example. Her eyes were full of feeling when she looked at me yesterday, but today they're dull and cold.'

I suggested that it might be the effect of the waters.

'You always see the worst side of things,' he said scornfully. 'Materialist! Still, let's talk of something more material.'

Pleased with this feeble pun, he quite cheered up.

Between eight and nine o'clock we went together to Princess Ligovskoy's. I saw Vera sitting at her window as we passed her house, and we exchanged a fleeting glance. Soon after we arrived she came into the drawing-room and the princess introduced me to her, saying she was a relative.

We had tea. There were a lot of guests, and the conversation was general. I tried to make myself agreeable to the old princess with my banter and several times had her laughing heartily. Once or twice Princess Mary was inclined to laugh as well, but controlled herself in order to keep up the pose she has adopted. She thinks that languor suits her, and she may well be right. Grushnitsky seems very pleased that she is immune to my gaiety.

After tea we all went into the drawing-room. As I passed Vera I asked her if she was satisfied with my obedience, and she gave me a loving look of gratitude. I'm used to these looks; though once they were the light of my life.

Princess Ligovskoy made Mary sit at the piano, and everyone asked her to sing, though I kept quiet and took advantage of the commotion to move to a window with Vera. She wanted to tell me something very important for both of us – pure nonsense, as it turned out.

Princess Mary was annoyed by my indifference. I could tell by the flashing look of anger she gave me. How well I understand this language of looks, mute but expressive, terse but emphatic.

She began singing. Her voice isn't bad, but she doesn't sing well – not that I listened. Grushnitsky, though, stood facing her, with his elbows on the piano, feasting his eyes on her and muttering all the time '*Charmant! Délicieux!*'[27]

'Listen,' said Vera. 'I don't want you to meet my husband, but you simply must make the princess like you. You'll find it easy enough, you can do anything you want to. This is the only place where we'll see each other.'

'The only place?'

She blushed.

'You know I'm your slave,' she said. 'I never could resist you, and I shall suffer for it: you will stop loving me. I want at least to keep my good name . . . not for my sake, you know that . . . Oh, please, please don't torment me the way you used to, raising false doubts and pretending not to care. I may die soon. Every day I feel myself getting weaker, but I still don't think of the life to come, I think only of you. You men don't know the joy that a look or a touch of the hand can give . . . Believe me, it's true. When I hear your voice I have such a deep, strange feeling of bliss that no kisses, however passionate, could ever give.'

By this time Princess Mary had stopped singing, and there was a general murmur of praise. I went up to her after everyone else and complimented her rather casually on her voice. She pulled a face, pouting her lower lip.

'Since you weren't even listening, I'm all the more flattered,' she said, with a mock curtsy. 'Perhaps you don't like music?'

'On the contrary, I do. Especially after dinner.'

'Mr Grushnitsky is right when he says your tastes are very prosaic – I see that music only appeals to you gastronomically.'

'You're wrong again. I'm no gastronome, in fact I've got a terrible digestion, but music after dinner sends me to sleep, and it's healthy to sleep – so music appeals to me medically. But in the evening it upsets me and makes me too sad or too jolly, and that's rather a bore when there's no special reason for it. Anyway, it's absurd to be sad in company, and it's improper to be too jolly . . .'

She walked away before I'd finished, and sat down by Grushnitsky. They embarked on a sentimental conversation, but though she tried to look as though she was listening, her answers to his sage remarks seemed rather vague and inappropriate, for now and then he looked at her in surprise, trying to guess the cause of the inner agitation that occasionally showed in her uneasy glances.

But I see what your game is, Princess, so beware! You want to pay me back, to wound my pride, but you won't succeed. Declare war on me, and I'll show you no mercy.

I tried to break into their conversation several times during the evening, but she greeted my remarks with reserve, and in the end I withdrew, pretending to be annoyed. She was triumphant, Grushnitsky too. Enjoy your triumph while you can, my friends – it'll be short-lived.

What will the outcome be? I've a good idea. With all the women I've ever met I've known for sure if they would love me or not.

I spent the rest of the evening with Vera and had my fill of talking over old times. I really can't think why she is so fond of me, especially since she's the only woman who's ever properly understood me and all my petty weaknesses and unhealthy passions. Can evil be so attractive?

I left at the same time as Grushnitsky. He took my arm when we were outside, then, after a long pause, said:

'Well, what do you think?'

I felt like telling him he was an idiot, but restrained myself and merely shrugged my shoulders.

29 May

The last few days I've stuck firmly to my plan. Princess Mary is beginning to enjoy my conversation. I've told her of some of the strange events in my life and she's coming to regard me as someone out of the ordinary. I make fun of everything, feelings especially, and this is beginning to alarm her. When I'm there, she doesn't venture into any sentimental discussions with Grushnitsky, and several times she's smiled ironically at things he's said. However, when Grushnitsky comes up to her, I always put on a humble look and leave them to themselves. The first time I did so she was pleased, or tried to pretend she was. The second time she was annoyed with me. The third time with Grushnitsky.

'You think very little of yourself,' she told me yesterday. 'Why do you think I prefer Grushnitsky's company to yours?'

I said I was sacrificing my own pleasure for the happiness of a friend.

'You're sacrificing mine as well,' she retorted.

I gazed at her with a serious look on my face – and then went the whole day without speaking to her. Last night she looked pensive, this morning at the well even more so. When I came along she was vaguely listening to Grushnitsky rhapsodizing about nature, but as soon as she saw me she started laughing, quite inappropriately, and pretended not to notice me. I walked on and watched her surreptitiously. Twice she turned away from Grushnitsky and yawned. No doubt about it, she's fed up with him. I'll go two more days without speaking to her.

3 June

I often wonder why I'm trying so hard to win the love of a girl I have no desire to seduce and whom I'd never marry. Why this womanish coquetry? Vera loves me more than Princess Mary will ever love anybody. If she were some unattainable beauty I might have been attracted by the difficulty of the undertaking. But that isn't the case, so it can't be that restless urge for love we suffer from in youth, that drives us from one woman to the next till we meet one who can't abide us. That's when our constancy begins, our true never-ending love that might be described mathematically by a line stretching from a point into space. The reason for this endlessness is simple: we can never attain our goal – our end, that is.

Why do I bother? Is it envy of Grushnitsky? Poor fellow, he's got nothing to envy. Or am I possessed by that vile, but irresistible urge which makes us destroy another's fond illusions for the petty satisfaction of saying to him, when he asks in desperation what he *can* believe in: 'My dear fellow, the same thing happened to me, but, as you see, I dine well, sup well, sleep soundly, and hope to succeed in dying without any cries and tears.'

And yet there's boundless pleasure to be had in taking possession of a young, fresh-blossomed heart. It's like a flower that breathes its sweetest scent to the first rays of the sun. You must pluck it at once, breathe your fill of its scent and cast it on the roadway to be picked up, perchance, by another. I've an insatiable craving inside me that consumes everything and makes me regard the sufferings and joys of others only in their relationship to me, as food to sustain my spiritual powers.

I'm no longer capable of losing my head in love. Ambition has been crushed in me by circumstances, but it comes out in another way, for ambition is nothing more than a lust for power and my chief delight is to dominate those around me. To inspire in others love, devotion, fear – isn't that the first symptom and the supreme triumph of power? To cause another person suffering or joy, having no right to do so – isn't that the sweetest food of our pride? What is happiness but gratified pride? If I thought myself better and more powerful than everyone else in the world, I should be happy. If everyone loved me I should find inexhaustible founts of love within myself. Evil begets evil. The first time we suffer, we see the pleasure to be had from torturing others. The idea of evil cannot enter a man's mind without his wanting to fulfil it in practice. Someone has said that ideas are organic creations, that the moment they are conceived they have form, this form being action. The most active man is the one who conceives most ideas, and so a genius stuck in an office chair must either die or go mad, and, in the same way, a man of strong physique who leads a sedentary and temperate life will die of apoplexy.

Passions are merely ideas in their initial stage. They are the property of youth, and anyone who expects to feel their thrill throughout his life is a fool. Tranquil rivers often begin as roaring waterfalls, but no river leaps and foams all the way to the sea. Tranquillity, however, is often a sign of great, if hidden, power. Intensity and depth of feeling and thought preclude wild outbursts of passion; in pain and pleasure the soul takes careful stock of all, and sees that so it must be. It knows that without storms the constant heat of the sun would dry it up. It gets steeped in its own existence, coddles and chides itself like a loved child. Only this higher state of self-knowledge can give man a true appreciation of divine justice.

Reading over this page, I see that I've wandered a long way from the point. It doesn't matter. After all, I'm writing this journal for myself, and anything I care to put in it will one day be a precious memory for me.

*

Grushnitsky came in and threw his arms round me – he's got his commission. We had some champagne, then Werner arrived.

'I won't congratulate you,' he said to Grushnitsky.

'Why not?'

'Because you look very well in your private's greatcoat, and you've got to admit that a line officer's uniform made by the local tailor isn't going to do anything for you at all. Don't you see? Up to now you've been an exception, but now you'll be just one of the common run.'

'Say what you like, Doctor, you won't stop me being pleased,' said Grushnitsky, adding in a whisper to me: 'He doesn't know what hopes these epaulettes give me. These wonderful epaulettes, with their stars, their lode-stars! Yes, now I am utterly happy.'

I asked if he would join us on the walk to the Chasm.[28]

'No fear,' he said. 'I'm not going to let the princess see me before my uniform is ready.'

'Shall I tell her about your good fortune?'

'No, please don't. I'd like it to be a surprise.'

'Tell me, though – how do things stand between you two?' I said.

He was confused and looked thoughtful. He hadn't the face to brag and lie, as he'd have liked to, but at the same time it was humiliating to admit the truth.

'What do you think?' I asked. 'Is she in love with you?'

'In love with me? Really, Pechorin, what ideas you have! How could it happen so quickly? Anyway, even if she is in love, no respectable woman would ever say so.'

'Oh, fine. And I suppose you think a respectable man must keep quiet about his love too?'

'Come now, my dear fellow. There's a way for everything. There's a lot you can guess without being told.'

'True. But the love we see in a woman's eyes commits her to nothing, while words ... But have a care, Grushnitsky. She's making a fool of you.'

'What, she?' he exclaimed, looking heavenwards and smiling complacently. 'I pity you, Pechorin.'

With that he left.

In the evening a large party set off on a walk to the Chasm. Many local scholars consider this Chasm to be, in fact, the crater of an extinct volcano. It is situated on the slopes of Mashuk, three-quarters of a mile from the town. A narrow track leads up to it through scrub and rocks.

Going up the hill, I gave my arm to Princess Mary, and she held on to it for the rest of the walk. First, we talked scandal. I went through all our acquaintances, present and absent, pointing out their comic features, then their bad ones. I was in a jaundiced mood, and though I began in jest, I was being really spiteful at the end. She was amused to begin with, but then frightened.

'You're a dangerous man,' she said. 'I'd rather fall victim to a cut-throat's knife in the forest than to your tongue. Seriously, though, if you ever decide to speak ill of me, I'd rather you took a knife and killed me. I fancy you'd not find it all that hard.'

'Am I really like a murderer, then?'

'No, you're worse.'

I was pensive for a moment, then, putting on a look of deep emotion, said:

'Yes, that's been my lot ever since I was a boy. Everyone saw in my face evil traits that I didn't possess. But they assumed I did, and so they developed. I was modest, and was accused of being deceitful, so I kept to myself. I had a strong sense of good and evil; instead of kindness I received nothing but insults, so I grew resentful. I was sullen, while other children were gay and talkative. I felt superior to them, and was set beneath them, so I became jealous. I was ready to love the whole world, but no one understood me, so I learned to hate. I spent my blighted youth in conflict with myself and the world. Fearing ridicule, I hid my best feelings deep within me, and there they died. I spoke the truth, but no one believed me, so I took to deceit. Knowing the world and the mainsprings of society, I became adept at the art of living. Yet I saw that others were happy without that art, enjoying for nothing the advantages I'd worked so hard to gain. That led me to despair, not the despair you can cure with a pistol barrel, but a cold, impotent despair that hid behind an affable exterior and a genial smile. I became a moral cripple. One half of my soul had ceased to exist. It had withered and died, so I cut it off and cast it away. But the other half was still active, living for the service of others. But no one noticed it, because no one knew of the dead half. But now you've reminded me of it – and I've pronounced its epitaph. Many people think epitaphs ridiculous, but I don't, especially when I think what lies beneath them. But I don't ask you to share my opinion. If you find what I've said absurd, by all means laugh. It won't distress me in the least, I can assure you.'

Our eyes met at this moment. Hers were welling with tears, her hand trembled on my arm, her cheeks were flushed . . . She pitied me! Sympathy, that feeling which preys so easily on women, had sunk its claws into her innocent heart. The whole walk she was preoccupied and didn't even flirt with anyone, and that's a great sign.

When we reached the Chasm, the ladies separated from their

escorts, but she didn't leave my arm. She was unamused by the quips of the local dandies and unalarmed by the steepness of the drop beneath us, though the other girls squealed and shut their eyes.

On the way back I didn't renew our sad conversation. To my idle questions and jokes she replied tersely, absently. In the end I asked if she had ever been in love.

She looked hard at me, then shook her head and again was lost in thought. She obviously wanted to say something but didn't know how to begin. Her bosom heaved – small wonder, for a muslin sleeve is poor protection against the electric impulse that was passing from my arm to hers. Most love-affairs begin this way. We often fool ourselves by thinking that a woman loves us for our physical or moral qualities. They pave the way, of course, they dispose her heart to receive the sacred fire, but it's the first physical touch that really counts.

When we got back, she forced a smile and said:

'I've been very amiable today, don't you think?'

We parted.

She's dissatisfied with herself, reproaches herself for being cold. This is the first triumph, the one that counts. Tomorrow she'll want to make it up to me. But I know it all by heart – that's the bore of it.

4 June

I saw Vera today. She tormented me with her jealousy. Apparently, Princess Mary has taken it into her head to confide to her the secrets of her heart. An excellent choice, I must say!

'I can tell the way things are going,' Vera said. 'Why don't you tell me now that you love her?'

'And what if I don't love her?' I said.

'Then why do you pursue her, upset her, arouse her imagination? Oh, I know you too well. Listen, if you want me to believe you, come to Kislovodsk[29] next week. We're going there the day after tomorrow. The princess is staying on here for a while. Take the house next to ours. We'll be staying in the big house by the spring, in the mezzanine. Princess Ligovskoy will be on the floor below us. There's a house next door owned by the same man that's not yet taken. Will you come?'

I promised, and the same day sent word that I wished to rent this house.

At six Grushnitsky came round with the news that his uniform would be ready tomorrow, just in time for the ball.

'At last I'm going to have a whole evening dancing with her. There are so many things I want to tell her, and now's my chance.'

'When is the ball?'

'Why, tomorrow. Surely you know that? It's a great event, being put on by the local authorities.'

'Coming for a stroll on the boulevard?' I asked.

'No fear, not in this beastly greatcoat.'

'Not so fond of it now, eh?'

I went out alone. I met Princess Mary and engaged her for the mazurka at the ball. She seemed surprised and pleased.

'I thought you only danced from necessity, like the last time,' she said, smiling very prettily.

She doesn't seem to have noticed Grushnitsky's absence.

'You'll have a pleasant surprise tomorrow,' I said.

'What's that?'

'It's a secret. You'll see for yourself at the ball.'

That evening I finished up at the Ligovskoys. The only other guests were Vera and an old man who was very entertaining. I was in a good mood and told them a number of improbable stories made up on the spur of the moment. Princess Mary sat facing me, listening to this nonsense with such profound, rapt, even tender attention that my conscience troubled me. What's become of her vivacity, her coquetry, her caprices, the haughty manner, the disdainful smile, the absent look?

Vera saw all this. She sat in the shadow by the window, sunk in a large armchair, looking ill and utterly miserable. I felt sorry for her.

Then I told the whole dramatic story of our relationship, of our love, naturally using fictitious names. I gave such a vivid description of my love and all its cares and raptures, and presented her character and actions in such a favourable light that she couldn't but forgive my flirting with Princess Mary.

She got up and came to sit with us and her spirits improved. It wasn't until two in the morning that we remembered the doctor's orders to go to bed at eleven.

5 June

Half an hour before the ball Grushnitsky came round, resplendent in his infantry officer's uniform. He had a *lorgnette* dangling from a bronze chain on the third button of his tunic, and wore enormous epaulettes that turned upwards like Cupid's wings, and boots that squeaked. He had his cap and brown kid gloves in his left hand and with his right kept arranging the ringlets of his carefully curled forelock. He looked pleased with himself, but somewhat diffident too. His festive appearance and grand bearing would have been enough to make me laugh outright, if that had suited my intentions.

He tossed his cap and gloves on the table and stood in front of the mirror, pulling down the tails of his tunic and straightening his dress. He wore an enormous black neckcloth on a high stiffener, the padding of which propped up his chin. He thought the inch or so of neckcloth showing above his collar wasn't enough, so tugged it up till it reached his ears. These exertions left him purple in the face, for his tunic collar was extremely tight and uncomfortable.

'I hear you've been busy making eyes at my princess lately,' he said casually, without looking at me.

'Where are fools like me to get a drink of tea!' I answered, repeating the favourite saying of one of the artfullest rogues of former times, whose praises Pushkin once sang.[30]

'Well, how do you think my uniform fits?' he asked. 'Ah, that damned Jew has made it too tight under the arms. By the way, do you have any scent?'

'Come off it,' I said. 'What do you want more scent for? You reek of rose-water as it is.'

'I don't care. Let's have some.'

He poured half a bottle down his cravat and on his handkerchief and sleeves.

'Are you going to dance?' he asked.

'I don't expect so.'

'I'm afraid I might have to lead with Mary in the mazurka, and I hardly know a single figure,' he said.

'Have you asked her for the mazurka?'

'No, I haven't yet.'

'Mind someone doesn't get in first.'

'Lord, you're right!' he said, slapping his forehead. 'Goodbye – I'll go and wait for her at the entrance.'

He snatched up his cap and hurried off.

I left half an hour later. The streets were dark and empty, but there was a crowd outside the Assembly Rooms (or tavern, if you prefer it). The windows were a blaze of lights, and strains of the regimental band came to me on the evening breeze. I walked slowly, feeling depressed.

Is it my sole function in life, I thought, to be the ruin of other people's hopes? Through all my active life fate always seems to have brought me in for the *dénouement* of other people's dramas. As if nobody could die or despair without my help. I've been the indispensable figure of the fifth act, thrust into the pitiful role of executioner or betrayer. What was fate's purpose? Perhaps I was meant to be a writer of bourgeois tragedies[31] or novels of family life, or a purveyor of stories, perhaps, for the *Reader's Library*?[32] How can one tell? Many people start life expecting to end up as

Alexander the Great or Lord Byron, then spend their whole lives as titular councillors.[33]

Entering the ballroom, I took refuge among a cluster of men and sized up the situation. Grushnitsky stood by Princess Mary, talking with great fervour. She listened inattentively, looking this way and that, her fan against her lips. She looked impatient, her eyes were seeking someone. I quietly went up behind them to hear what they were saying.

'Princess, you're tormenting me,' said Grushnitsky. 'You've changed a lot since I last saw you.'

'You've changed as well,' she said, darting him a glance whose hidden mockery was lost on him.

'I change? Never! You know that's impossible. Anyone who sees you once must carry your divine image with him to the grave.'

'Oh, do stop it!'

'A short while ago you listened kindly when I said these things to you, and often too. Why won't you listen now?'

'Because I dislike repetition,' she laughed.

'Oh, I've been sadly mistaken. Fool that I was, I thought at least that with these epaulettes I'd have the right to hope. But no, I'd be better off in my contemptible greatcoat. Perhaps that was why you noticed me.'

'Indeed, I really do think your greatcoat suited you much better.'

At this point I went up and bowed to the princess. She blushed slightly, then said quickly:

'Monsieur Pechorin, don't you think Monsieur Grushnitsky looked much nicer in his grey greatcoat?'

'No, I don't agree,' I replied. 'His uniform makes him look more boyish than ever.'

This shot was too much for Grushnitsky. Like all boys, he fancies himself an old man. He thinks the deep lines of passion on his face pass muster for the stamp of age. With a furious look at me, he stamped and walked away.

'Confess, though,' I said to the princess. 'He's always been ridiculous, but it's not so long since you found him – and his greatcoat – interesting, is it?'

She looked down and made no reply.

The whole evening Grushnitsky pursued her, dancing either with her or *vis-à-vis*, devouring her with his eyes, sighing, and pestering her with pleas and reproaches. By the end of the third quadrille she hated him.

'I never expected this from you,' he said, coming up and taking me by the arm.

'Never expected what?'

'You're dancing the mazurka with her, aren't you?' he asked in a solemn voice. 'She's admitted it to me.'

'Well, what of it? It's not a secret, is it?'

'Of course not. I should have expected as much from a flirt, a minx like her. But I'll get even.'

'Why blame her? Blame it on your greatcoat or your epaulettes. She can't help it if she doesn't like you any more.'

'Then why did she raise my hopes?'

'Why did you hope? I can understand someone wanting a thing and trying to get it, but who ever hopes?'

'You've won your bet,' he said, with a vicious smile. 'Only not quite.'

The mazurka began. Grushnitsky picked Princess Mary every time, and she was constantly chosen by others too, so there was obviously a plot against me. So much the better – she wants to talk to me and they won't let her, so she'll want to twice as badly.

I squeezed her hand a couple of times. The second occasion she drew it away without saying anything.

'I shall sleep badly tonight,' she told me at the end of the mazurka.

'That's Grushnitsky's fault.'

'Oh no, it's not,' she said.

She looked so sad and thoughtful that I promised myself I'd kiss her hand before the evening was out.

People began to leave. As I handed the princess into her

carriage, I quickly pressed her tiny hand to my lips. It was dark, so no one could see.

I went back to the ballroom, well pleased with myself.

The young bloods were having supper at the big table. Grushnitsky was there. Evidently they were talking about me, for when I went in they all stopped. A lot of them have it in for me since the last ball, especially the dragoon captain, and now they seem to be ganging up against me in earnest, with Grushnitsky as ringleader. He's looking very proud and courageous.

I'm delighted. I love enemies, though not in the Christian way. They amuse me, stir my blood. Being always on the alert, catching their every glance, the hidden meaning of every word, guessing their next step, confounding their plans, pretending to be taken in and then with one fell blow wrecking the whole elaborate fabric of their cunning schemes – that's what I call living!

All through supper Grushnitsky was whispering and exchanging winks with the dragoon captain.

6 June

This morning Vera left for Kislovodsk with her husband. I met their carriage on my way to the Ligovskoys. She nodded to me. She looked reproachful.

Whose fault is it? Why won't she give me an opportunity of seeing her alone? Love is like fire – without fuel it dies. Perhaps jealousy will succeed where pleas have failed.

I spent a whole hour at the Ligovskoys, but Mary didn't appear because she is unwell. She wasn't out on the boulevard this evening either. There's a gang of them formed, armed with *lorgnettes*, and they look menacing. I'm glad Princess Mary is ill, or else they might have insulted her in some way. Grushnitsky is looking dishevelled and has a desperate air. He seems genuinely put out, especially on account of his wounded vanity. But then, in some people even despair is amusing.

I reached home with the feeling that something was missing. *I hadn't seen her. She's ill.* Perhaps I've fallen in love myself? What nonsense!

7 June

At eleven this morning (the hour when Princess Ligovskoy is usually sweating it out in the Yermolov baths)³⁴ I passed their house. Princess Mary was sitting at the window, lost in thought. On seeing me, she jumped up.

I went into the hall. There were no servants about, so I took advantage of the easy-going customs of these parts and made my way to the drawing-room unannounced.

Princess Mary stood by the piano. One hand, trembling slightly, rested on the back of an armchair. Her charming face looked matt and pale. I went slowly up to her.

'Are you angry with me?' I asked.

She looked up at me with a deep, languid gaze, then shook her head. She wanted to speak, but couldn't. Tears filled her eyes, and, covering her face, she sank into the chair.

'What's wrong?' I asked, taking her hand.

'You don't respect me . . . Oh, leave me alone!'

I took a few steps . . . She sat up straight in her chair, her eyes shining. I stopped, with my hand on the door-handle.

'Forgive me, Princess,' I said. 'I behaved like a madman. It won't happen again: I'll see to it . . . There's no reason for you to know what's been going on in my heart. You'll never know, and so much the better for you. Good-bye.'

As I left I thought I heard her crying.

I wandered about in the neighbourhood of Mashuk till evening. I was extremely tired, and when I got home I fell on my bed in a state of utter exhaustion.

Werner dropped in to see me.

'Is it true you're going to marry Princess Mary?' he asked.

'Why do you ask?'

'It's all over the town. All my patients are full of this important news. And there's no one like my patients for knowing everything.'

Grushnitsky is up to his tricks, I thought.

'To prove how untrue these rumours are, Doctor, I'll let you into a secret. I'm leaving for Kislovodsk tomorrow.'

'Princess Ligovskoy as well?'

'No. She's here for another week.'

'You can't be getting married then!'

'Come now, Doctor. Look at me. Do I look like a man who's about to be married or anything like it?'

'I'm not saying you do. But,' he added, with a sly smile, 'there are cases . . . when an honourable man is obliged to marry, and some fond mothers do not, to say the least, prevent this happening. So I advise you as a friend to watch your step. The air in these spas is extremely dangerous. I've seen a lot of fine young men who deserved a better fate going straight from here to the altar. Would you believe it – they even tried to marry me off once! It was one of those provincial mothers. Her daughter was a pale creature, and I had the misfortune to say that marriage would soon bring the colour back to her cheeks, whereupon the mother wept with gratitude and offered me the girl's hand and her entire fortune – fifty serfs,[35] I think it was. But I said I wasn't cut out for it.'

Werner left, fully convinced that he had saved me by his warning.

From what he had said I saw that ugly rumours were being put about the town concerning Princess Mary and myself. Grushnitsky won't get away with that!

10 June

I've been in Kislovodsk three days now. Each day I see Vera at the well and out walking. When I wake up in the morning, I sit by the window and look at her balcony through my glass. She is already dressed, waiting for the prearranged signal. We meet as though by chance in the garden that goes down from our houses to the well. She has got back her colour and strength in this invigorating mountain air. It's not for nothing that they call Narzan 'the heroes' spring'.[36] The local people claim that the air in Kislovodsk puts one in the mood for love, and that love affairs that begin at the foot of Mashuk[37] reach happy endings here. There is certainly an all-pervading air of solitude about the place. Everything is mysterious: the murky shade of the lime walks above the foaming torrent that roars down from ledge to ledge, cutting its way through the green-clad hills, and the ravines, full of mist and silence, that branch off here in all directions, the freshness of the scented air, heavy with the perfume of tall southern grasses and white acacia, and the ceaseless, lusciously soporific sound of icy streams that meet at the foot of the valley and merrily race one another till at last they rush into the Podkumok. On this side the gorge is broader, opening out into a green valley, with a dusty road winding along it. Every time I look at this road I fancy I see a carriage with a rosy face looking through the window. Many carriages have passed along the road, but not yet this one.

The suburb beyond the fort is now a populous district. There's a restaurant on the hill a few yards from my lodging, and in the evenings its lights glitter through the double row of poplars. The shouting and clinking of glasses goes on till all hours of the night.

More Kakhetian wine and mineral water are drunk here than anywhere else in the world.

> Many are fond of combining these two,
> But it's something that I prefer never to do.[38]

Grushnitsky and his gang have rowdy parties in the tavern each day. He scarcely bows to me now.

He only arrived yesterday and has already quarrelled with three old fellows who wanted to go before him at the baths. No doubt about it – misfortune is making him aggressive!

11 June

They've arrived at last. I heard their carriage as I sat at my window, and my heart missed a beat. What does it mean? Can I be in love? The stupid way I'm made, it's the sort of thing you might expect.

I dined with them. The princess looks very tenderly at me and keeps close to her daughter – a bad sign. Vera, on the other hand, is jealous of Princess Mary: I've attained this happy state. What won't a woman do to hurt a rival! I remember one woman who fell in love with me simply because I was in love with someone else. There's nothing more paradoxical than the female mind, and you can never convince a woman of anything – you have to arrange matters so that they convince themselves. The chain of reasoning they employ to overcome their own prejudices is extremely original, and if you want to master their dialectic you have to turn all the textbook rules of logic upside-down. For example, a normal approach would be: 'This man loves me, but I'm married, so I mustn't love him'. But a woman's approach would be: 'I mustn't love him, because I'm married, but he loves me, so . . .' I have to use dots here, for now the voice of reason is silent, and it's mainly the tongue, eyes and heart (if there is one) which do all the talking.

If a woman ever chances to read these notes there'll be outraged cries of 'Slander!'

Since poets began writing and women began reading them (for which our heartfelt thanks), they have been called angels so often that, in their simplicity, they've come to accept this compliment as the truth. They forget that the same poets – in return for money – acclaimed Nero[39] as a demigod.

I really oughtn't to be so biting about them, I who have loved nothing in the world but them and have always been ready to sacrifice for them peace of mind, ambition, even life itself. But it's not from pique or injured vanity that I attempt to pluck from them the magic veil that needs a practised eye to see through. No, all I say is just the result of

> The intellect's cold observations,
> The bitter record of the heart.[40]

Women should wish all men to know them as well as I do, for since I stopped fearing them and understood their petty weaknesses, I've loved them a hundred times more dearly.

Incidentally, the other day Werner compared women to the enchanted forest in Tasso's *Jerusalem Delivered*.[41]

'No sooner do you approach,' said he, 'than untold horrors swarm on you from every side – duty, pride, respectability, public opinion, ridicule, disdain. You mustn't take any notice of them, but just walk straight ahead. The monsters gradually vanish, and before you opens a peaceful, sunny glade, with the green myrtle blossoming in its midst. But all is lost, if your heart quakes and you turn back at the beginning.'

12 June

This evening was rich in events.

Two or three miles from Kislovodsk, in the gorge of the Podkumok, there's a rock called The Ring.[42] It stands high on a hill and forms a natural gateway, through which the setting sun casts a last fiery glance at the world. A large party of us rode out to watch the sunset through this stone window, though, in fact, nobody gave much thought to the sun.

I rode by Princess Mary, and on the way home we had to ford the Podkumok. Any mountain stream is dangerous to ford, even the shallowest of them, chiefly because of the way the bed shifts. It's like a kaleidoscope, changing every day with the force of the current, and where there is a rock one day, there will be a hole the next. I took the princess's horse by the bridle and led it into the water. It was only knee-deep, and we started slowly across, moving diagonally upstream. It's a well-known fact that you should never look down at the water when crossing a swift-flowing stream, or you'll feel giddy. I forgot to warn her about this.

When we were in mid-stream, where the current was fastest, she suddenly swayed in the saddle.

'I don't feel well,' she muttered feebly.

I quickly leaned across and put my arm round her supple waist.

'Look up,' I whispered. 'It's all right. Just don't be afraid. I'm here.'

She felt better and tried to free herself from my arm, but I tightened my grip on her soft, tender waist. My face was almost touching hers, and I could feel the warmth of her burning cheek.

'What are you doing to me?' she cried. 'Oh, God!'

Disregarding her trembling and confusion, I touched my lips on her tender cheek. She quivered, but said nothing. We were riding behind the others, so no one saw us. When we came out on the far bank, the whole party set off at a trot. The princess held her horse back, and I stayed by her. She was obviously disturbed by my silence, but I vowed that, out of curiosity, I would say nothing. I wanted to see how she would extricate herself from this awkward situation.

'Either you despise me or else you love me very much,' she said.

There were tears in her voice.

'Perhaps you wish to make fun of me, to rouse my feelings and then desert me, but that would be so base and vile, the very idea . . . No,' she added, her voice tender and trusting, 'there's really no reason why you shouldn't respect me, is there? I must forgive your boldness, for I allowed it to happen. Say something! Answer me! I want to hear your voice.'

There was so much feminine impatience in these last words that I couldn't help smiling. Luckily it was getting dark.

I made no reply.

'You are silent?' she said. 'Perhaps you want me to say first that I love you?'

I said nothing.

'Is that what you want?' she asked, turning sharply towards me. There was something terrifying in the resolute expression of her face and voice.

I shrugged my shoulders.

'Why should I?' I answered.

She lashed her horse and galloped full tilt along the narrow, perilous track. It happened so quickly that I barely managed to catch up with her, and by then she had rejoined the main party.

All the way home she talked and laughed. There was a feverish quality in her movements. She ignored me completely. Everyone noticed her unusually high spirits, and her mother was inwardly delighted to see her daughter like this, though in fact it was just a state of nerves. She'll be awake all night crying. The thought gives me enormous satisfaction. There are times when I can understand the Vampire,[43] and yet I still pass for a decent fellow and try my best to be thought so.

The ladies dismounted and went into the Ligovskoys. I was feeling on edge, so galloped into the hills to clear my head of the thoughts that crowded in on me. There was a heady coolness in the dewy evening air. The moon was rising over the dark peaks, and my unshod horse's every step echoed dully through the silence of the valleys. I gave my horse a drink by a waterfall, took a couple of deep breaths of the cool southern night air and set off home.

I went by way of the suburb. The lights were going out in the windows, and the sentries on the wall of the fort exchanged long drawn out shouts with Cossacks in the neighbouring pickets.

I noticed one house built on the edge of a ravine which was particularly brilliantly lit. Occasional shouts and a babble of voices told me it was an officers' drinking party.

I dismounted and crept up to a window. One shutter was not properly closed and I could see the people inside and hear what they said. They were talking about me. The dragoon captain, flushed with wine, banged his fist on the table for order.

'Gentlemen!' he said. 'It's just not good enough. We've got to teach Pechorin a lesson. These Petersburg puppies get above themselves unless you slap them down. Just because he's got clean gloves and polished boots he fancies he's the only society man among us.'

'Yes, with that superior smile of his!' said another. 'Actually, I think he's a coward, nothing more than a coward.'

'I think so too,' said Grushnitsky. 'He likes passing everything off as a joke. I once said things to him anyone else would have killed me for on the spot, but he just made a joke of it. Naturally I didn't challenge him – that was up to him to do, and anyway I didn't want to get involved.'

'Grushnitsky's got it in for him because he cut him out with the princess,' remarked someone.

'That's rich!' said Grushnitsky. 'It's true, I did show some interest in her, but I soon gave up. I'm not keen to get married, and I don't believe in compromising a girl.'

'You take my word,' said the dragoon captain. 'He's a prize coward – Pechorin, I mean, not Grushnitsky. Grushnitsky's a fine fellow and my very good friend. So, gentlemen, there's nobody here who stands up for him? Nobody? So much the better. Would you like to see how brave he is? It'll be a bit of sport for us.'

'By all means. How?'

'Now, listen. Grushnitsky's got a special grievance against him, so he takes the lead. He'll take him up on some trifle and challenge him to a duel. Just a minute – this is the whole point . . . He'll challenge him, fine. Challenge, preparations, conditions – all very solemn and awesome, I'll see to that. I'll be your second, my poor friend. All right. Only here's the catch – we won't put bullets in the pistols. I guarantee Pechorin will funk it. Damn it, I'll fix the duel at six paces. Are you with me?'

There was general agreement.

'Splendid scheme! We're game! Why not?'

'What about you, Grushnitsky?'

I waited quivering for his reply. The thought that but for chance I might have become the laughing-stock of these fools filled me with cold malice. If Grushnitsky had refused to agree I would have embraced him, but after a short silence he rose, stretched out his hand to the captain and replied pompously:

'Very well, I agree.'

It would be hard to describe the delight of the worthy company.

I went home, stirred by two quite different emotions. The first was sorrow. Why do they all hate me? I thought. What cause have they? I haven't offended anyone, have I? Or am I one of those people the very sight of whom rouses hostility? And I felt my heart slowly filling with venomous spite.

'Take care, Grushnitsky,' I said, pacing my room. 'You don't play that kind of trick on me, and you may find yourself paying dearly for going along with your stupid friends. I'm not your plaything.'

I was awake all night, and by morning I was as yellow as parchment.

I met Princess Mary at the well during the morning. She studied me closely.

'Are you ill?' she asked.

'I didn't sleep last night,' I said.

'Neither did I. I was blaming you, perhaps unfairly? Please tell me. I can forgive everything.'

'Everything?'

'Yes, everything. Only now tell me the truth, please. I've thought a lot about it, I've tried to explain and justify your behaviour. Are you afraid of difficulties from my family? That doesn't matter. When they know' – her voice quivered – 'I'll talk them round. Or is it your position?[44] Please understand, I'm ready to sacrifice everything for the man I love. Oh, please answer me, please. Have pity on me. You don't despise me, do you?'

She seized my hand.

Her mother was walking ahead of us with Vera's husband. She saw nothing, but we were in full view of the invalids out walking, and there's no one worse than invalids for prying and gossiping about other people's affairs. I quickly withdrew my hand from her passionate grip.

'I'll tell you the whole truth,' I said. 'I'll not defend myself or explain my actions. I do not love you.'

Her lips paled slightly.

'Leave me,' she said, her voice barely audible.

I shrugged my shoulders, turned and walked away.

14 June

Sometimes I despise myself – perhaps that's why I despise others? I've lost my capacity for noble impulses, for I'm afraid of making a fool of myself. Anyone else would have offered the princess *son cœur et sa fortune*,[45] but for me the word 'marriage' has a magic power. However passionately I might love a woman, the first hint that she expects me to marry her banishes my love for good. My heart turns to stone, its warmth gone for ever. I'll make any sacrifice except this one. I'll hazard my life, even my honour, twenty times, but I will not sell my freedom.

Why do I value it so much? What use is it to me? What am I preparing myself for? What do I expect from the future? In fact, nothing at all.

I have this innate fear, this uncanny premonition. After all, some people are unaccountably afraid of spiders, cockroaches and mice. Perhaps I should admit it – that when I was a child an old woman told my mother my fortune and said I would die through a bad wife. I was deeply impressed by this at the time and acquired this unconquerable aversion to marriage. Something tells me her prophecy will come true, but at least I'll do what I can to delay it.

15 June

Apfelbaum[46] the conjurer arrived here yesterday. A long poster appeared on the door of the restaurant informing the respected public that the above-named remarkable conjurer, acrobat, alchemist and illusionist would have the honour to present a spectacular performance this day at eight o'clock p.m. in the hall of the Assembly Rooms (alias the restaurant). Tickets 2 roubles 50 copeks.

Everyone is going to watch the remarkable conjurer, and even Princess Ligovskoy has bought a ticket, although her daughter is unwell.

I walked past Vera's windows after dinner. She was sitting alone on the balcony, and a note dropped at my feet.

Come this evening after nine. Use the main stairs. My husband has gone to Pyatigorsk and won't be back till morning. The servants and maids will all be out – I've given them tickets for the show. I've done the same for the princess's servants. I'm expecting you. You must come.

Aha! I thought, things have turned my way at last.

At eight I went to see the conjurer. It was nearly nine when the audience had assembled and the show began. I spotted Vera's servants and the princess's in the back rows. They were all there. Grushnitsky was sitting in the front row with his *lorgnette* and every time the conjurer wanted a handkerchief, watch, ring, and so on, he applied to him.

Grushnitsky has been cutting me for some time, and now he gave me a couple of rather insolent looks. It will all be in the record when we come to settle our account.

A little before ten I got up and left.

It was pitch black outside. The mountains all round were capped by cold, heavy clouds, and a dying wind rustled occasionally in the tops of the poplars round the restaurant. People crowded at the windows.

I went down the hill and, quickening my pace, turned into the gate. I had a sudden feeling there was someone following me. I stopped and looked back, but saw nothing in the darkness. Still, to be on the safe side, I walked right round the house as though I were out for a stroll. As I passed Princess Mary's windows I again heard steps behind me and a man muffled in a greatcoat ran past me. Despite this alarm, I crept to the porch and hurried up the dark stairway. The door opened, a small hand grasped mine.

'Did anyone see you?' Vera whispered, pressing herself to me.

'No, nobody.'

'Now do you believe that I love you? I was in torment making up my mind, but you can twist me any way you want.'

Her heart was thumping, her hands were like ice. She came out with a string of jealous reproaches and complaints. She wanted me to make a clean breast of everything and said she would resign herself to my being unfaithful, since all she wanted was my happiness. I didn't altogether believe her, but comforted her with vows, promises and the rest.

'So you're not going to marry Mary?' she said. 'You don't love her? But she thinks . . . Do you know the poor girl's madly in love with you?'

*

At about two in the morning I opened the window and with two shawls knotted together let myself down from the upper balcony to the one below, steadying myself on a pillar. There was still a light in Princess Mary's room and, on impulse, I went up to her window. The curtain wasn't quite drawn, so I could cast a curious glance inside. Mary was sitting on the bed, her hands folded on her lap. Her thick hair was gathered up under a lace-trimmed night-cap. She had a large crimson shawl over her shoulders and gaily-coloured Persian slippers on her tiny feet. She sat quite still, her head sunk on her breast. A book lay open on the table before her, but her fixed, sorrowful eyes seemed to be reading the same page for the hundredth time, with her thoughts far away.

At this moment someone stirred behind a bush. I leaped from the balcony on to the grass.

'Aha, got you!' cried a rough voice. 'I'll teach you to go visiting princesses at night!'

'Hold him tight!' cried a second person, springing out from the corner.

It was Grushnitsky and the dragoon captain.

I laid out the dragoon with a punch on the head and dashed into the bushes. I knew every path of these gardens on the slope opposite our houses.

'Thieves! Help!' they cried, and there was a musket shot – the smoking wad landed almost at my feet.

A minute later I was in my room, undressed and in bed. My servant scarcely had the key turned in the lock when Grushnitsky and the captain banged on my door.

'Pechorin!' roared the captain. 'Are you asleep? Are you there?'

'I'm in bed,' I called back angrily.

'Well, get up. There are thieves about, Circassians . . .'

'I've got a bad cold,' I said. 'I don't want to catch a chill.'

They went away. I shouldn't have answered and then they could have spent another hour looking for me in the garden.

Meanwhile, there was a frightful state of alarm. A Cossack came galloping down from the fort, and there was a general bustle of activity, with people searching for Circassians behind every bush – naturally without success. Many, however, were probably quite convinced that if only the garrison had shown more pluck and dash, then a good score of the raiders would have been laid low.

16 June

At the well this morning the sole subject of conversation was the night raid of the Circassians. When I'd had my quota of Narzan and taken a dozen turns along the lime walk, I met Vera's husband, just back from Pyatigorsk. He took my arm and we went to lunch at the restaurant. He was very concerned about his wife.

'She was terrified last night,' he said. 'Of course it would happen just when I was away.'

We sat down to lunch by the door into a side room where a dozen of the young set had gathered. Grushnitsky was there, and once again I was destined to overhear a conversation which was to settle his fate. He'd not seen me, so I couldn't suppose he acted by design, though this only made him the more culpable as far as I was concerned.

'Was it really Circassians, though?' someone asked. 'Did anybody see them?'

'I'll tell you the whole thing,' said Grushnitsky. 'Only please don't say I told you. What happened was this: last night a certain person, whose name I won't mention, came and told me he'd seen someone getting into the Ligovskoys' house some time after nine. The old princess was here, you will note, but the daughter was at home. So we went and waited for this lucky fellow under her window.'

I confess I was alarmed. Though my companion was engrossed in his lunch, he might well hear some rather distasteful facts if Grushnitsky happened to have realized the truth. But Grushnitsky was blinded by jealousy and never suspected what had really happened.

'So along we went,' he continued. 'We took a gun loaded with blank, just to put the wind up him. We waited in the garden till two and then somebody came down from the balcony, I don't know where from — it wasn't through the window because it didn't open. He probably came out of the glass door behind the pillar. Anyway, down he came. What do you think of the princess now, eh? These Moscow princesses really are the limit. What can you believe after this, eh? We tried to grab him, but he got away and hared off among the bushes. That was when I fired at him.'

There were incredulous murmurs.

'So you don't believe me?' said Grushnitsky. 'Well, I give you my solemn word of honour it's the absolute truth. If you like I can prove it by telling you the man's name.'

'Come on then, tell us. Who is he?' they cried.

'Pechorin.'

At that moment he looked up and saw me facing him in the doorway. He flushed crimson. I went up to him and said slowly and clearly:

'I'm sorry I didn't come in before you staked your honour on this disgusting slander. My presence might have stopped you acting basely for once in your life.'

Grushnitsky leaped up with a show of fury, and I continued in the same tone:

'I ask you to take back what you've said this instant. You know very well it's pure invention, and I don't think a woman's indifference to your brilliant qualities merits this terrible revenge. Think seriously what it means. You stand by what you said, and you lose the right to be called a man of honour – and are in danger of your life.'

Grushnitsky stood in front of me, eyes downcast, in a state of violent emotion. The struggle between conscience and conceit didn't last long, however. The dragoon captain, sitting next to him, nudged him with his elbow. Grushnitsky started, and then, with his eyes still lowered, hastily replied:

'When I say a thing, sir, I mean it and am ready to repeat it. I'm not afraid of your threats and I'll go to any lengths . . .'

'That you've already demonstrated,' I retorted icily.

Then, taking the dragoon captain's arm, I left the room.

'What do you want?' asked the captain.

'You're Grushnitsky's friend,' I said. 'I presume you'll be his second?'

He made a solemn bow.

'You're quite correct,' he said. 'In fact, I'm obliged to be his second, since your insult to him is also an insult to me – I was with him last night in the garden,' he added, pulling his drooping figure erect.

'Ah, so it was you I gave that clumsy punch on the head?' I said.

His face turned yellow, then blue with stifled rage. I pretended not to notice his fury and said:

'I shall have the honour to send you my second today.'

I met Vera's husband on the restaurant steps. He seemed to be waiting for me and grasped my hand in a state of near rapture. When he spoke there were tears in his eyes.

'Noble fellow!' he said. 'I heard it all. That ungrateful scoundrel! What decent man's going to have him in his house after that? Thank heaven I have no daughters! You'll get your reward, though, from the lady you're risking your life for. In the meantime you can rely on my discretion. I was young myself once and a military man too. I know one mustn't interfere in these affairs. Good-bye.'

The poor fool. He's glad he has no daughters!

I went straight to Werner's and found him in. I told him the whole story, all about me and Vera and Princess Mary, and about the conversation I had overheard when they were planning to dupe me into fighting a duel with pistols loaded with blank. They wanted to make a fool of me then, but now it was past a joke. They probably never expected it to turn out like this.

The doctor agreed to be my second, and I gave him instructions about the terms of the duel. He was to insist on the utmost secrecy, for though I'm prepared at any time to risk being killed, I'm not in the least disposed to ruin my future prospects in this world.

I went home. An hour later Werner was back from his errand.

'There's a plot against you, all right,' he said. 'I found that dragoon captain at Grushnitsky's, and another fellow, I can't remember his name. I stopped a moment in the hall to take off my galoshes and heard them arguing and making a frightful row. "I absolutely refuse," Grushnitsky was saying. "He's insulted me in public. Before it was different." "You won't be concerned in it," said the captain. "I'll see to everything. I've been a second in five duels and know how to fix it. I've got it all worked out, so just leave it to me. There's no harm in giving him a fright, and why risk danger yourself if you don't have to?"'

'I went in at this point and they all stopped talking. Our discussions took some time, but this is what we decided on in the end. There's a lonely gorge three miles or so from here. They're going there at four o'clock tomorrow morning and we'll leave half an hour after them. You'll fire at six paces – that was Grushnitsky's own idea – and if either of you is killed we put it down to the Circassians. Now, I'll tell you what I suspect. I think they – the seconds – have changed their original plan and are going to load Grushnitsky's pistol with ball, but not yours. It smacks of murder, but this is war, Asian war at that, and no holds are barred. Grushnitsky seems to have a bit more decency than his friends, though. Well, what do you think? Should we let them know we're on to it?'

'Not on your life, Doctor. Don't you worry, they won't get the better of me.'

'What are you going to do?'

'That's my secret.'

'Well, see you don't get caught. It's at six paces, you know.'

'Doctor,' I said, 'I'll expect you tomorrow at four. The horses will be ready. Good-bye.'

I stayed in till evening, locked in my room. A servant came from the Ligovskoys' asking me to call on the old princess, but I told him to say I was unwell.

It's two in the morning. I can't sleep, though I ought to get some sleep if I'm to have a steady hand in the morning. Still, it's difficult to miss at six paces. Ah, Grushnitsky, your ruse won't work. The roles will be reversed – it'll be I who studies your pale face for the marks of hidden fear. Why did you choose these fatal six paces? Do you think I'll meekly be your target? Oh no, we'll draw lots and then . . . then . . . What if your luck holds out against mine? What if my star lets me down at last? It might well do, for it's pandered to my whims long enough, and there's no more constancy in heaven than on earth.

What if it does? If I die, I die. It will be small loss to the world, and I've had about enough of it myself. I'm like a man yawning at a ball who doesn't go home to bed because his carriage hasn't come. But when it arrives – farewell!

I've been going over my past, and I can't help wondering why I've lived, for what purpose I was born. There must have been some purpose, I must have had some high object in life, for I feel unbounded strength within me. But I never discovered it and was carried away by the allurements of empty, unrewarding passions. I was tempered in their flames and came out cold and hard as steel, but I'd lost for ever the fire of noble endeavour, that finest flower of life. How many times since then have I been the axe in the hands of fate? Like an engine of execution, I've descended on the heads of the destined victims, often without malice, but always without pity. My love has brought no one happiness, for I've never sacrificed a thing for those I've loved. I've loved for myself, for my own pleasure, I've only tried to satisfy a strange inner need. I've fed on their feelings, love, joys and sufferings, and always wanted more. I'm like a starving man who falls asleep exhausted and sees rich food and sparkling wines before him. He rapturously falls on these phantom gifts of the imagination and feels better, but the moment he wakes up his dream disappears and he's left more hungry and desperate than before.

And perhaps tomorrow I'll die, and then there'll be no one who could ever really understand me. Some will think me worse, others better than in fact I am. Some will say I was a good fellow, others that I was a scoundrel. Neither will be right. So why bother to live? One just goes on living out of curiosity, waiting for something new. It's absurd and annoying.

*

I've now been six weeks here in the fort at N—. Maxim Maximych has gone out hunting, and I'm alone, sitting by the window. There are grey clouds right down to the foot of the mountains and the sun is just a yellow blob shining through the mist. It's cold, and there's a whistling wind that rattles the shutters. I'm bored, so I'll go on with my journal that's been interrupted by so many strange events.

It's funny to read over the last page. I thought I might die. But that was impossible – even now I've not yet drained my cup of suffering, and feel I still have long to live.

How clearly and sharply the past is etched in my memory. Not a single line or detail has been erased by time. I remember not sleeping a wink the night before the duel. I couldn't write for long, for I had a strange feeling of disquiet. I spent an hour pacing the room, then sat down and opened a novel that lay on the table. It was Walter Scott's *Old Mortality*.[47] At first it was an effort to read, but I was soon carried away by the magic of the tale. The Scottish bard must surely be rewarded in heaven for every moment's pleasure given by his book.

At last it grew light. My nerves were steady now. I looked in the mirror: there was a dull pallor on my face, which still bore the marks of my wretched sleepless night. My eyes, though, shone proud and hard, despite the dark rings round them. I was satisfied with myself.

I ordered the horses to be saddled, then got dressed and went quickly down to the baths. I immersed myself in the cold bubbling Narzan water and felt my physical and mental strength return.

I came out of the bath feeling fresh and spry, I might have been preparing for a ball. Now try telling me that the soul doesn't depend on the body!

When I got back I found Werner in my rooms. He wore grey

breeches, a short topcoat and a Circassian cap. I burst out laughing at the sight of his tiny frame beneath this enormous shaggy cap. There was nothing warlike about his face at the best of times and on this occasion it looked even longer than usual.

'Why so sad, Doctor?' I asked. 'You've seen scores of people into the next world without turning a hair, haven't you? Pretend I've got a bilious fever. I might recover, or I might just as easily die: one thing or the other, it's all in the way of nature. Try to think of me as a patient with a disease you've never met before, and you'll find it most absorbing. Now's your chance to make some interesting physiological observations on me. Don't you think the expectation of violent death is really a kind of malady?'

He was interested in this idea and cheered up.

We mounted and set off, with Werner clinging to the reins with both hands. In no time we had galloped past the fort, through the suburb and into the gorge along which the road twisted. The road was half overgrown with tall grass and continually crossed by a rushing stream, which had to be forded – much to the doctor's dismay, since each time his horse stopped in the water.

I can't remember a bluer, fresher morning. The sun was just peeping over the green mountain-tops, and its first warmth, mingling with the dying cool of the night, filled me with a delicious sense of ease. The joyful rays of the new day had not yet reached into the gorge and gilded only the topmost crags that overhung us on either side. The least puff of wind showered us with silver rain from the thick leafy bushes growing in the deep folds of the cliffs. I loved nature then, I remember, more than ever before. With what fascination I studied each trembling dewdrop on the broad vine leaves that reflected a million multicoloured rays. How eagerly my eyes tried to see into the hazy distance, where the road grew ever narrower and the cliffs bluer and more fearsome, till at last they appeared to join in one impenetrable wall.

We rode in silence.

'Have you made your will?' asked Werner suddenly.

'No. I've not.'

'What if you're killed?'

'The heirs will show up all right.'

'Have you no friends you'd like to send a last farewell?' he asked.

I shook my head.

'No woman even you'd like to leave a keepsake for?'

'Do you want me to open my heart to you, Doctor?' I said. 'I'm past the age when a man dies with his sweetheart's name on his lips and leaves his best friend a lock of hair (pomaded or otherwise). When I think of possible, imminent death, I think only of myself. Some people don't even do that. To hell with the friends who'll forget me in a day or, worse, tell a lot of fantastic tales about me, and the women who'll lie in another man's arms and ridicule me to stop him being jealous of the dear departed. The turmoil of life has left me with a few ideas, but no feelings. For a long time now I've lived by intellect, not feeling. I weigh and analyse my emotions and actions with close interest, but complete detachment. There are two men within me – one lives in the full sense of the word, the other reflects and judges him. In an hour's time the first may be leaving you and the world for ever, and the second? . . . the second? . . .'

'Look, Doctor, there on the right. Do you see those three figures on the cliff? That'll be our opponents, I think.'

We spurred our horses to a trot.

Three horses were tethered in the bushes at the foot of the cliff. We tethered ours by them and made our way up a narrow path to the ledge where Grushnitsky was waiting for us with the dragoon captain and his other second, who was called Ivan Ignatievich – I never heard his surname.

'We've been waiting for you a long time,' said the dragoon captain, smiling ironically.

I took out my watch and showed it to him. He apologized and said his watch must be fast.

For a while there was an awkward silence, broken finally by Werner, who said to Grushnitsky:

'Now that you've both shown you're ready to fight and honour's satisfied, I think you might come to terms and end the affair amicably.'

'I'm willing,' I said.

The captain winked at Grushnitsky and Grushnitsky, imagining that I was backing out, put on a very haughty look, though till then he'd been looking very pale. For the first time since our arrival he looked at me, and I saw his face was troubled and showed signs of inner conflict.

'State your conditions,' he said. 'You can be sure I shall do all I can . . .'

'My conditions are these: you make an immediate public withdrawal of your slander and apologize to me.'

'You astonish me, sir, that you dare to propose such things.'

'What else could I propose?'

'Then we'll fight.'

I shrugged my shoulders.

'Just as you like. But remember – one of us will certainly be killed.'

'I hope it's you,' he said.

'I'm sure it won't be.'

Grushnitsky blushed in confusion and gave a forced laugh.

The captain took him by the arm and led him aside. They whispered together for a long time. I had arrived in a fairly pacific frame of mind, but I was beginning to be infuriated by all this. Werner came up to me, plainly disturbed.

'Look,' he said. 'You seem to have forgotten all about their plot. I don't know how to load a pistol, but as things are . . . You're a strange man. If you tell them you know what they're up to, they'll never dare . . . What's the point of being shot down like a bird?'

'Please don't worry. Doctor,' I said. 'Just wait. I'll see they have no unfair advantage. Let them whisper.'

Then I said in a loud voice:

'Gentlemen, we're getting tired of waiting. If we're going to fight, then let's get on with it. You had time enough to talk yesterday.'

'We're ready,' said the captain. 'Take your places, gentlemen. Doctor, will you kindly measure out six paces?'

'Places, gentlemen,' echoed Ivan Ignatievich in a piping voice.

'Just a minute,' I said. 'I've one more condition. As we're fighting to the death we must do all we can to keep it a secret and see that our seconds aren't held responsible. Do you agree?'

'Yes, certainly.'

'Well, here's what I've thought. You see that narrow shelf up there on the right at the top of the sheer cliff? It must be a good two hundred foot drop to those jagged rocks at the bottom. If each of us stands on the edge of that shelf when the other fires, then even a slight wound will be fatal. This must accord with your wishes, since it was you who chose to fight at six paces. If one of us is wounded he'll be bound to go over and be dashed to pieces. The doctor will take out the bullet and his death can easily be put down to an unlucky fall. We'll draw lots to see who fires first. And let me finish by saying that I'll not fight on any other terms.'

'As you wish,' said the captain, with a meaning look at Grushnitsky, who nodded his agreement.

Grushnitsky's face was a mixture of expressions. I had put him in an awkward situation. Under normal conditions he could have aimed at my legs, given me a slight wound and had his revenge without overburdening his conscience. But now he had either to fire wide or else become a murderer – or, in the last resort, abandon his cheap trick and run the same risk as myself. I shouldn't have cared to be in his shoes at that moment.

He took the captain aside and spoke to him very heatedly. I noticed his lips were blue and trembling. But the captain turned away with a smile of contempt, and said quite loudly:

'You're a fool. You don't understand at all. Shall we go, gentlemen?'

A narrow path led through the bushes up the sheer cliff, a

tottering natural stairway of broken rocks. Clinging to the bushes, we started scrambling up the slope. Grushnitsky led the way, followed by his seconds, then the doctor and me.

'You're an astonishing fellow,' said the doctor, shaking me firmly by the hand. 'Let's feel your pulse. Ha, feverish! It doesn't show in your face, though, except for a brightness in the eyes.'

There was a sudden loud rush of stones under our feet. It was Grushnitsky – he'd missed his footing when the branch he was holding broke. He would have gone sliding down on his back if his seconds hadn't supported him.

'Careful!' I shouted. 'Don't fall too soon. It's a bad omen – remember Julius Caesar.'[48]

We had now reached the top of this jutting cliff. The ledge was covered with fine sand and might have been prepared for a duel. There were mountains all round, their peaks jostling together like an enormous flock of sheep, fading into the golden morning haze. The massive white shape of Elbrus towered in the south, at the end of the chain of icy peaks. Wispy clouds blowing in from the east drifted through the mountains.

I went to the edge of the shelf and looked down. My head almost reeled. Below me it was dark and cold as the grave, and jagged, moss-covered rocks, brought down by time and storms, awaited their prey.

The ledge on which we were to fight was almost a perfect triangle. Six paces were measured from the projecting corner, and it was agreed that the first to face the other's fire should stand on the edge of this corner, his back to the precipice. If he weren't killed, we should change places.

I decided to give Grushnitsky every advantage. I wanted to test him. He might show a spark of decency after all, and then all would be well. But his weakness and vanity were bound to prevail, and I wanted to have every right to show him no mercy if fortune spared me. Who has never made such bargains with his conscience?

'Toss, Doctor,' said the captain.

Werner took a silver coin from his pocket and held it up.

'Tails!' cried Grushnitsky hastily, like a man suddenly woken by a friendly shove.

'Heads!' said I.

The coin spun up and fell with a ring to the ground. We all rushed to see it.

'You're lucky,' I said to Grushnitsky. 'You get first shot. But remember this – if you don't kill me, I promise I shan't miss.'

He flushed. He was ashamed to kill an unarmed man. I looked hard at him. For a moment I thought he was going to fall at my feet and beg my forgiveness, but how could he admit to having had such base intentions? There was only one course left to him – to fire wide. I was sure that's what he would do! The only thing that might put him off was the thought that I would ask for a second duel.

Werner tugged my sleeve.

'Now's the time,' he said. 'You must tell them now that we know what they're about, or you're done for. Look, he's already loading. If you won't say anything, I'll tell them myself.'

'Don't do that, Doctor, whatever you do,' I said, holding him back by the arm. 'You'll spoil everything. You promised not to interfere. Why should you worry? I might want to be killed.'

He looked at me in surprise.

'Oh well,' he said, 'that's different. Only don't blame me when you're dead.'

The captain had now finished loading the pistols and gave one to Grushnitsky, smiling and whispering something as he did so, and the other to me.

I stood on the corner of the ledge, bracing my left leg firmly against a stone and leaning slightly forward to avoid toppling backwards if I got a slight wound. Grushnitsky stood opposite me and at the given signal raised his pistol. His knees were shaking, but he aimed straight at my forehead.

I seethed with fury.

Suddenly he lowered the muzzle of his pistol and turned to his second, white as a sheet.

'I can't do it,' he said in a hollow voice.

'Coward!' retorted the captain.

A shot rang out. The bullet grazed my knee, and I involuntarily took a few steps forward to get away from the edge of the cliff.

'A pity you missed, Grushnitsky, old boy,' said the captain. 'It's your turn now, so take your place. Embrace me first, though. We'll never meet again.'

They embraced, the captain scarce able to keep a straight face.

'Never fear,' he said, with a sly look at Grushnitsky. 'The world's a fool, fortune's a whore, and life's a bore.'

Having uttered this tragic statement with due solemnity, he went back to his place, and then, after a tearful embrace from Ivan Ignatievich, Grushnitsky was left facing me alone. I still can't define the feeling that surged in my breast at that moment. It was a combination of contempt, injured pride, and spite at the thought that two minutes before this man who regarded me now with such assurance and calm effrontery had, risking nothing himself, tried to kill me like a dog – for if the wound in my leg had been any worse, I'd have certainly gone over the cliff.

For a few moments I stared him hard in the face to see if there was the least sign of remorse, but I got the impression he was suppressing a smile.

'I suggest you say your prayers before dying,' I said.

'Don't worry more about my soul than you do about your own,' he answered. 'I only ask that you get on and fire your shot.'

'So you won't take back your slander? You won't apologize? Think carefully. Have you nothing on your conscience?'

'Mr Pechorin!' cried the dragoon captain. 'Let me remind you that you're not here to hold confessions. Let's get it over with. Somebody might come along the gorge and see us.'

'Very well,' I said. 'Doctor, would you come over here, please.'

He came over. Poor Werner, he was whiter than Grushnitsky had been ten minutes before.

I then spoke the following words, loudly, clearly and distinctly, the way one pronounces a death sentence.

'Doctor, these gentlemen have forgotten to put a bullet in my pistol. Through haste, I suppose. Would you mind loading it again? And make a good job of it.'

'Impossible!' cried the captain. 'Impossible! I loaded both of them. Your bullet may have rolled out, but you can't blame me for that. Anyway, you've got no right to reload, no right at all. It's quite against the rules. I won't allow it.'

'Very well,' I said. 'In that case you and I will fight on the same terms.'

That silenced him.

Grushnitsky stood with bowed head, sullen and embarrassed.

'Oh, let them be!' he finally said to the captain, who was trying to snatch my pistol from Werner. 'You know they're right.'

The captain made signs to him, but Grushnitsky wouldn't even look.

Meanwhile, the doctor loaded the pistol and handed it to me. Seeing this, the captain spat and stamped his foot.

'You're a fool, my friend,' he said, 'a common fool. If you put me in charge, then you should do just what I say. Serves you right! Go ahead, die like a fly!'

He turned and walked away, muttering 'Anyway, it's against the rules.'

'Grushnitsky,' I said, 'there's still time. Take back your slander, and I'll forgive you everything. You failed to make a fool of me, so my pride is satisfied. Remember, we used to be friends . . .'

His face flared, his eyes flashed.

'Shoot!' he said. 'I despise myself and hate you. If you don't kill me, I'll slit your throat some night. The world's too small for both of us.'

I fired.

When the smoke cleared Grushnitsky was not on the ledge. There was a faint swirl of dust hanging over the edge of the cliff. Everyone cried out.

'*Finita la commedia*,'[49] I said to Werner.

He made no reply and turned away in horror.

I shrugged my shoulders and, with a bow to Grushnitsky's seconds, I left.

As I went down the path I saw Grushnitsky's blood-stained body among the clefts in the rocks. I involuntarily closed my eyes.

I untethered my horse and set off slowly home. My heart was like lead, the sun seemed to have lost its brightness, and I felt no warmth from its rays.

Before I got to the suburb I turned right, along the valley. I was sick of the sight of humanity and wanted to be alone. I dropped the reins and rode for a long time with my head sunk on my chest and in the end found myself in a place I didn't know at all. I turned my horse back and set about finding the way; the sun was already setting when, exhausted, I reached Kislovodsk on my exhausted horse.

My servant said Werner had called and he handed me two notes, one from Werner, the other from Vera.

I opened Werner's note first. It ran as follows:

It's all gone as well as it could. The body was brought in badly disfigured and with the bullet taken out of his chest. Everyone believes he died accidentally. Only the commandant (who probably knew of your quarrel) shook his head, but said nothing. There's no evidence against you, so you may sleep in peace – *if you can*. Good-bye.

I hesitated a long time before opening the second note. What could Vera be writing to me for? I was filled with foreboding.

This is the letter. Every word is stamped indelibly on my memory.

I am writing to you in full certainty we shall never meet again. I thought the same when we parted a few years back, but heaven chose to test me once more. I failed, because my feeble heart once more obeyed the familiar voice. You won't despise me for that, will you?

This will be a farewell letter and confession in one. I must tell you all that has built up inside me since I first loved you. I shan't blame you – you treated me as any other man would have done, you loved me as a chattel, a thing to provide you with the joys, fears and sorrows without which life is dull and tedious. I realized that at the start, but you were unhappy and I sacrificed myself, hoping that one day you would appreciate my sacrifice and understand the depth of my love for you, come what may. That was a long time ago. Since then I've seen you through and through and realized my hope was vain. I was miserable, but now my love was part of me: it faded, but didn't die.

We are parting now for ever. But rest assured, I shall never love anyone else. My heart has given all it had, all its tears and hopes to you. A woman who has once loved you will always feel disdain for other men – not because you are better, no, but because there's something special in you that others haven't got, something proud and mysterious. Whatever you say, your voice has an irresistible power. No one is so persistent in his desire for love. In no one is evil so attractive. No one promises so much happiness in a look. No one knows better how to use his advantages. And no one can be so genuinely unhappy as you, because no one tries so hard to persuade himself that he isn't.

Now I must tell you why I'm leaving in such a hurry. You'll think it a trivial reason, for it concerns only me.

My husband came this morning and told me about your quarrel with Grushnitsky. My face must have shown what I felt, for he stared at me for a long time. I nearly fainted when I thought of your fighting today, and all on account of me. I thought I'd go mad, but now that I can think about it, I'm sure you won't be killed. You'll never die without me! My husband walked up and down the room for a long time. I don't know what he said, I can't remember what I answered, I probably told him that I love you. All I remember is that in the end he abused me and called me a dreadful name, then left. I heard him order the carriage.

I've been sitting by the window for three hours now, waiting for you to come back. But you are alive, you cannot die.

The carriage is almost ready. Good-bye. I'm ruined – but what do I care? If I could be certain that you'll always remember me – not love, just remember . . .

Good-bye. There's someone coming – I must hide this letter . . .

You don't really love Mary, do you? You're not going to marry her? You must make this sacrifice for me, do you hear? I've lost everything for you.

I rushed out to the steps like a madman, leaped on my horse that was being walked round the yard, and galloped like the wind along the Pyatigorsk road. I spurred my weary horse unmercifully, and it sped me along the stony road, snorting and lathered with sweat.

The sun had disappeared in a black cloud that rested on the ridge of mountains to the west, and in the valley it was dark and dank. The Podkumok threaded its way through the boulders with a dull monotonous roar.

I galloped, breathless with impatience. The thought of arriving in Pyatigorsk too late to catch Vera hammered at my heart. If only I could see her for one more minute, to say goodbye, to press her hand . . . I prayed, cursed, wept, laughed. I can't describe the state of agitation and despair I was in. Now that I might lose her for ever Vera was dearer to me than anything else in the world – life, honour, happiness. God alone knows what unlikely, crazy schemes rushed through my mind.

Still I galloped on, spurring my horse without mercy, till suddenly I noticed his laboured breathing. Twice he stumbled, though the going was good. It was still three miles to Yessentuki,[50] a Cossack village where I could get another mount, and if my horse held out for ten more minutes, all would be well. But, rising from a gulley at the end of the mountains, we took a sharp bend and he suddenly crashed to the ground. I sprang from the saddle and pulled the reins to try and get him up, but it was no good. He gave a faint groan through his clenched teeth and a few minutes later was dead. I was left alone in the steppe, my last hope gone. I tried walking, but my legs gave way beneath me.

Worn out by the excitements of the day and my sleepless night, I fell down on the wet grass and wept like a child.

I lay there a long time, weeping bitterly, not attempting to hold back the tears and sobs. I thought my chest would burst. All my coolness and self-control vanished like smoke, my heart wilted, reason deserted me. Anyone seeing me at that moment would have turned away in contempt.

When the night dew and mountain breeze had cooled my burning head and I could think clearly again, I saw how futile and senseless it was to pursue lost happiness. What more did I want? To see her again? For what? Wasn't it all over between us? One painful farewell kiss would add nothing to my memories and would only make parting more difficult.

Still, it's nice to know I'm capable of tears! Though perhaps it was the result of strained nerves, a sleepless night, a couple of minutes looking into the barrel of a pistol, and an empty stomach.

It's all for the best. This new suffering has, in military jargon, 'created a successful diversion'. Crying is good for you, and if I hadn't gone off riding and been forced to walk ten miles back, I should probably have had another sleepless night. But as it was, I got back to Kislovodsk at five in the morning, threw myself on my bed and slept like Napoleon after Waterloo.

It was dark outside when I woke. I sat by the open window and unbuttoned my caftan. The mountain breeze cooled my breast, which the deep sleep of fatigue had failed to calm. Lights in the distant buildings of the fort and the suburb across the river glittered through the tops of the thick limes that shaded its banks. Outside all was quiet. The princess's house was in darkness.

Werner came in. He was frowning and didn't offer his hand as he usually did. I asked him where he'd been.

'At Princess Ligovskoy's. Her daughter's ill, a nervous disorder. That's not what I've come about, though. Look, the authorities are putting two and two together, and even if they can't prove anything definite I advise you to watch your step. The princess has just told me she knows you fought over her daughter.

That old chap told her all about it – what's his name? – he saw your brush with Grushnitsky in the restaurant. I came to warn you. Good-bye. We mightn't meet again – they're liable to send you away.'

He stopped in the doorway. He wanted to shake hands, and if I'd shown the least inclination to do so, he'd have thrown his arms round me. But I remained stone cold, and he left.

People! They're all the same: they know all the bad sides of a thing before you do it, they help, advise, and, when they see there's no other way, they even approve of it – then afterwards they wash their hands of it and turn away in disgust from the man who's had the guts to take all the burden of responsibility. They're all the same, even the best and cleverest of them.

Next morning I was ordered by the authorities to proceed to the fort at N—. I went to say good-bye to Princess Ligovskoy.

She asked if I had anything specially important to say to her and was surprised when I only said that I wished her well, etc.

'I must have a serious talk with you,' she said.

I sat down without speaking.

She obviously didn't know how to begin. She turned red in the face, her puffy fingers drummed on the table, then in the end she began in a broken voice:

'Look, Monsieur Pechorin. I believe you to be an honourable man.'

I bowed.

'In fact, I'm sure you are, though your behaviour has been rather dubious. There may be reasons for it that I don't know about, and you must tell me now what they are. You've defended my daughter's name, you fought and risked your life on her account. Don't say anything – I know you won't admit it, because Grushnitsky has been killed.' She crossed herself. 'God forgive him – and you as well, I hope. For my part, I daren't condemn you, for my daughter was the innocent cause of it all. She has told me everything – or so I think. You told her you love her, and she confessed as much to you.' She gave a deep sigh. 'But she's ill, and I'm sure this is no ordinary illness. Some secret sorrow is killing her. She won't admit it, but I'm sure that you're the cause of it.

'You may think I'm looking for rank or wealth – think nothing of the sort. All I want is my daughter's happiness. Your present situation is an unenviable one, but it may improve. You're a man of means, my daughter loves you, and with her upbringing she'll make her husband a happy man. I am rich, and she is my only child. Tell me, what holds you back? I shouldn't be saying all this, but I trust in your heart, your honour – remember, I have but one daughter . . .'

She burst into tears.

'Princess,' I said. 'It is impossible for me to answer you. May I talk to your daughter alone?'

'Never!' she cried, rising from her chair in great agitation.

'As you wish,' I said, and made ready to go.

After a moment's thought she motioned me to wait and left the room.

Some minutes passed. My heart was pounding, but my head was cold and my mind calm. Try as I might, I couldn't find the least spark of love in me for charming Mary.

The door opened and she came in. Heavens, how she'd changed since last I saw her, such a short while before.

As she reached the middle of the room she swayed. I leaped up and helped her to an armchair.

I stood facing her. There was a long silence. Her big eyes were filled with an inexpressible sorrow and seemed to search in mine for anything akin to hope. Her pale lips made a vain effort to smile, and her delicate hands, folded in her lap, looked so thin and transparent that I pitied her.

'Princess,' I said. 'You know I was making sport of you. You must despise me.'

An unhealthy flush spread over her cheeks.

'And so,' I went on, 'you cannot love me . . .'

She turned away, rested her elbows on the table and covered her eyes. I thought I saw the glint of tears.

'My God . . .' she exclaimed, her voice barely audible.

This was getting too much for me — another minute and I'd have fallen at her feet.

'So you can see for yourself,' I said in as firm a voice as I could muster, and forcing a grin, 'It's obvious I can't marry you. Even if you wanted this now, you'd soon regret it. It's my talk with your mother that makes me speak so openly and bluntly now. I hope she's mistaken — you can easily make her think otherwise. You see me playing a mean and despicable part — I confess it is so; that is all I can do for you. However badly you think of me, I submit to your view. See how I debase myself — even if you loved me, you'd despise me now, wouldn't you?'

She turned to me, pale as marble, but with a glorious spark in her eyes.

'I hate you,' she said.

I thanked her, bowed respectfully and walked out.

An hour later I was bowling along the road from Kislovodsk in the mail. Two or three miles from Yessentuki I saw the body of my fiery steed by the roadside. The saddle was gone, probably taken by some passing Cossack, and two ravens sat in its place on the horse's back. I sighed and turned away. PARADOX

Now that I'm stuck here in this fort I often think back and wonder why I didn't choose to follow the path that fate had opened to me, where there were quiet joys and peace of mind in store for me. I could never have settled to it, though. I'm like a sailor, born and bred on the deck of a privateer. Storm and battle are part of his life, and if he's cast ashore he pines in boredom, indifferent to the pleasures of shady woods and peaceful sunshine. All day long he walks the beach, listening to the steady murmur of the incoming waves and gazing for the sight of a ship in the distant haze. He looks longingly at the pale strip between the ocean blue and the grey clouds, in hopes of seeing a sail, first like a seagull's wing, that then gradually stands out against the foaming breakers and runs in steadily towards the desolate haven.

3

The Fatalist

Once I had to spend a couple of weeks in a Cossack village on the left flank. There was an infantry battalion stationed there, and each night the officers met at someone's quarters for an evening of cards.

On one occasion we sat up late at Major S——'s. We'd tired of playing boston[1] and tossed the cards under the table. For once we had an interesting conversation – we were talking about the way many Christians accept the Muslim belief that a man's destiny is written in heaven, and everyone had some strange story to tell for or against.

'All this proves nothing, gentlemen,' said the old major. 'You quote all these odd incidents to back up your views, but none of you actually saw them happen.'

'Of course not,' said many, 'but we heard them from reliable witnesses.'

'Rubbish!' said someone. 'Where are the reliable witnesses who have seen the list with the hour of our death on it? If predestination really exists, why have we been given free-will and reason? Why do we have to give an account of our deeds?'

At this point an officer who was sitting in the corner got up and walked slowly to the table. He surveyed us with a look of calm dignity.

Lieutenant Vulich was a Serb by origin, as you could tell from his name, and his looks matched his character perfectly. He was tall, dark-complexioned, with black hair and black, piercing

148

eyes; he had the large, though straight nose common to his race, and a cold, sad smile played perpetually on his lips. All this combined to make him seem like someone apart, unable to share his thoughts and feelings with those into whose company he was thrown.

He was brave, spoke little, but had a sharp tongue. He never spoke to anyone about his personal or domestic life; he drank scarcely at all, and never ran after the Cossack girls – whose charms have to be seen to be believed. There was talk that the colonel's wife was not indifferent to his soulful eyes, but he always got extremely angry if anyone mentioned it.

There was only one passion he didn't conceal, and that was his passion for gambling. At the card table he was oblivious of everything. He usually lost, but his constant lack of success only made him more persistent. It was said that one night on a sortie he was keeping the bank on his pillow and having a terrific run of luck. Suddenly there were shots, the alarm was sounded and everyone jumped up and rushed for their weapons. But Vulich didn't move.

'Stake for the lot!' he called to one of the most ardent punters.

'The seven,' replied the punter, hurrying away.

Oblivious of the general confusion, Vulich finished the deal, and a seven came up. When he reached the firing line shots were flying thick and fast, but Vulich didn't bother about the bullets and swords of the Circassians and sought out the lucky punter. He finally spotted him among the riflemen, who were beginning to force the enemy out of the wood.

'The seven turned up,' he called, then went up to him, took out his purse and wallet and presented them to the winner, ignoring his objections about the inopportuneness of the moment. With this disagreeable task out of the way, Vulich had charged forward at the head of some soldiers and kept up a cool fire against the Circassians till the engagement ended.

We all stopped speaking when Vulich came up to the table, for everyone imagined he'd do or say something unusual.

'Gentlemen,' he said, his voice calm, though lower than usual. 'Gentlemen, what's the point of this futile arguing? You want to know if a man disposes of his own life or if his last hour is preordained. I suggest we try it out on ourselves. Who's game?'

There were shouts of 'Not me!' 'What a crazy idea!'

'What about a bet?' I asked, jokingly.

'What on?' said Vulich.

'I say there's no such thing as predestination,' I said, tipping some twenty gold pieces on to the table, all that I had in my pocket.

'Taken!' said Vulich in a hollow voice. 'Major, would you be referee? Here are fifteen gold pieces. Would you mind adding the five you owe me?'

'Very well,' said the major. 'But I really don't see what it's all about or how you're going to settle it.'

Without a word Vulich went into the major's bedroom. We followed him. He went up to a wall with weapons on it and took down at random one of the pistols of different calibres hanging there. We still couldn't see what he had in mind, but when he cocked the pistol and primed the pan, there were several who cried out and caught him by the arms.

'What are you trying to do? You're mad!' they shouted.

He freed his arms and said slowly:

'Gentlemen, which of you will pay my twenty gold pieces?'

They all walked away in silence.

Vulich went back into the other room and sat at the table. We followed and he motioned us to sit down round him. We silently obeyed. He had acquired some mysterious power over us. I looked him hard in the eyes, but he met my searching gaze with a look of steady calm and a smile flickered on his pale lips. Yet, for all his composure, I fancied I saw the mark of death on his pale face. I've noticed it myself, and I've heard a lot of old soldiers say the same, that a strange mark of inevitable doom can often be seen on the face of a man a few hours before he dies. Anyone with an eye for it is rarely mistaken.

'You're going to die today,' I said.

He turned sharply towards me, but answered slowly and calmly: 'I might, I might not.'

Then he turned to the major and asked if the pistol was loaded, but the major was so perplexed that he couldn't rightly remember.

'Come off it, Vulich!' cried someone. 'It was hanging by the bed, so it's bound to be loaded. What's the point of joking?'

'It's just a silly joke,' said someone else.

'Fifty roubles to five the pistol's not loaded!' cried another.

Fresh bets were laid.

I'd had enough of all this.

'Look,' I said. 'Either shoot yourself or else put the pistol back and we'll go to bed.'

Many of the others agreed.

'Good idea. Let's go to bed,' they said.

'Gentlemen, please don't move,' said Vulich, putting the muzzle to his forehead. Everyone froze. Then he said:

'Pechorin, take a card and toss it up.'

I picked up a card from the table, I think it was the ace of hearts, and tossed it in the air. Everyone held their breath. With mingled fear and some indescribable curiosity, all eyes darted to and fro between the pistol and the fateful ace. It fluttered in the air and floated slowly down. As it touched the table, Vulich pulled the trigger. The pistol misfired.

There were cries of 'Thank God! It wasn't loaded.'

'Let's just see, though,' said Vulich, cocking it again and aiming at a cap hanging over the window. A shot rang out and the room filled with smoke. When it had cleared, the cap was taken down – there was a hole straight through the middle and the bullet was embedded in the wall.

For two or three minutes everyone was speechless, while Vulich calmly put my gold pieces in his purse. Then everyone started to explain why the pistol hadn't gone off the first time. Some said the pan had been dirty, others suggested in undertones that the powder was damp the first time and that Vulich had then added some fresh powder. But I said that this wasn't true, for I'd not once taken my eyes off the pistol the whole time.

'You've got gambler's luck,' I said to Vulich.

'For once in my life,' he said, smiling with satisfaction. 'This is better than faro or bank.'[2]

'Rather more dangerous, though.'

'Well, do you believe in predestination now?' he asked.

'Yes, I believe in it,' I said, 'but I can't understand why I was so sure you were going to die today.'

And this man who, just before, had been calmly pointing a pistol at his own forehead was now suddenly discomposed and flared up.

'That'll do!' he said, rising. 'Our bet's over now and you've no business saying things like that.'

He picked up his cap and left. It struck me as odd – and not without reason!

Soon everyone went home, each offering his own explanation of Vulich's eccentricities, and probably all agreeing that I'd been selfish to bet against a man who was going to shoot himself – as though he needed me to provide an opportunity!

I walked home through the empty back streets of the village. A full red moon was just showing over the broken line of buildings, like the glare of a fire. Stars shone calmly in the deep blue sky, and I was amused to think that there were once wise men who imagined the stars took part in men's petty squabbles over a patch of land or some imagined rights. While in fact these lamps, which they supposed had been lit for the sole purpose of shining down on their battles and triumphs, still burn on as bright as ever, while they, with all their passions and hopes, have long since vanished, like a fire lit by some carefree traveller at the edge of a forest. Yet what strength they derived from this certainty that the heavens with all their countless hosts looked down on them in silent, but never-failing sympathy. And we, their pitiful descendants, drift through the world without beliefs or pride, without pleasure or fear, except that instinctive dread that grips us when we think of our inevitable end. We can no longer make great sacrifices for the good of mankind, or even for our own happiness, because we know it is unattainable; and as our ancestors plunged on from illusion to illusion, so we drift indifferently from doubt to doubt. Only unlike them, we have no hope, nor even that indefinable but real sense of pleasure that is felt in any struggle, be it with men or with destiny.

Many similar thoughts ran through my mind, but I didn't dwell on them, for I'm not given to brooding on abstract ideas. It gets you nowhere. As a boy I was a dreamer and dwelt with loving care on the dark and radiant images traced by my restless, eager fancy. And what did it bring me? Weariness, as though I'd spent a night wrestling a phantom, and a vague, regretful memory. In this fruitless struggle I wasted all the ardour of spirit and firmness of will that are needed in real life; when I then came into this real life, I had lived it through already in my mind and found it boring and disgusting, like reading a poor pastiche of a long familiar book.

The events of the evening had made a considerable impression on me and set me on edge. I'm not sure now if I believe in predestination or not, but that evening I had no doubts of it at all. We'd had striking proof of it, and though I'd ridiculed our ancestors and their obliging astrology, I now found myself taking the same line. However, I stopped myself from going too far along this perilous path, and since I make it a rule never to reject absolutely or to put blind faith in anything, I turned from metaphysical speculations to attend to the ground under my feet. This proved a very timely precaution, for I tripped and almost fell over something plump and soft, though not, apparently, alive. The moon was shining straight on to the road, and I bent down to see what it was. Before me lay a pig sundered in two by sabre.

I'd barely had time to inspect it when I heard steps and saw two Cossacks come running out of a side-street. One of them came up and asked if I'd seen a drunken Cossack chasing a pig. I told them I'd seen no Cossack, but pointed to the unlucky victim of his reckless daring.

'The scoundrel!' said the second Cossack. 'He gets a skinful of *chikhir*[3] and then goes off on the rampage. Come on, Yeremeich, we'd better go after him and get him tied up, or he might . . .'

They went off, and I walked on, taking extra care, till I was safely home.

I was lodging with an old Cossack sergeant, a man I liked for his kindly nature and – more particularly – for his pretty daughter Nastya. She was waiting for me by the gate as usual, wrapped in a fur coat. In the moonlight I saw her sweet lips were chilled blue by the night air. She smiled when she saw me, but I was in no mood to stop. 'Goodnight, Nastya,' I said and walked past. She was going to reply, but only sighed.

I shut my door behind me, lit the candle and threw myself down on the bed. I was longer than usual going to sleep and there was a pale light in the eastern sky by the time I did get off. That night, however, I was *not* predestined to sleep undisturbed. At four in the morning a pair of fists pounded at my window. I leaped up to see what it was. There were shouts of 'Get up and get dressed.' I scrambled into my clothes and went outside.

Three officers had come for me. They were white as a sheet and all spoke at once.

'Do you know what's happened?'

'No,' I said. 'What?'

'Vulich has been killed.'

I was stunned.

'Yes, killed,' they said. 'Come on, quick!'

'Where are we going?'

'We'll tell you on the way.'

We set off, and they told me what had happened, interspersing their story with comments on the strange quirk of fate that had saved Vulich from certain death only half an hour before he had died. He'd been walking alone down the dark street when along came the drunken Cossack who had killed the pig. The fellow might have gone by without seeing him, if Vulich hadn't suddenly stopped and asked him who he was looking for. 'You!' said the Cossack, and struck him a blow with his sword that split him from the shoulder almost down to the heart. The two Cossacks I'd seen chasing the murderer had come along and picked up the wounded man, but he was on the point of death and said only three words: 'He was right'. I alone realized what these mysterious words meant – they referred to me, for I had unthinkingly foretold the poor fellow's death. My instinct hadn't failed me – I had in fact seen the mark of death in the changed look on his face.

We were making our way to an empty cottage at the end of the village where the murderer had locked himself in. Droves of wailing women were heading the same way, and an occasional Cossack dashed belatedly into the street, hastily buckling on his dagger and running on ahead of us. There was terrible confusion.

At last we arrived at the cottage. The doors and shutters were fastened from the inside. A crowd stood round, officers and Cossacks held heated discussions, women wailed and lamented. I was immediately struck by the expressive face of an old woman in the crowd who was looking frantic with despair. She sat on a thick log, her elbows on her knees, holding her head in her hands. It was the murderer's mother. Now and then her lips moved – it might have been a whispered prayer, or a curse.

Meanwhile we had to decide on some way of seizing him, but nobody was anxious to be the first in. I went up to the window and looked through the crack of the shutter. He lay on the floor, a pistol in his right hand, a blood-stained sword by his side. He was pale, his expressive eyes rolled furiously, and every now and then he shuddered and clasped his head, as though hazily recalling the events of the night. There seemed so little resolution in his troubled look that I told the major it would be better for the Cossacks to break down the door and go in now, rather than wait till he had come fully to his senses.

Just then an old Cossack captain went up to the door and called the murderer's name. He answered.

'You've done wrong, Yefimich,' said the captain. 'All you can do now is give yourself up.'

'I won't!' said the Cossack.

'Have a conscience, man. You're an honest Christian, aren't you, not some plaguey Chechen? If you do wrong, you must just face up to it and take what comes.'

'I won't do it!' cried the Cossack menacingly, and we heard the click of a pistol being cocked.

The captain spoke to the old woman.

'Here, Mother,' he said. 'Have a word with your boy. He might listen to you. He's only making it worse for himself with the Almighty, carrying on like this. And besides, he's been keeping these gentlemen standing about for two hours.'

The old woman stared at him and shook her head.

He went up to the major.

'He won't give himself up, sir,' he said. 'I know him. If we break in, he'll do for a good many of our lads. Would you like us to shoot him? The crack in the shutter's wide enough.'

Just then I had an odd idea. Like Vulich, I decided to put fate to the test.

'Half a minute,' I said to the major. 'I'll get him alive.'

I told the captain to engage him in conversation and posted three Cossacks by the door ready to smash it in and come to my aid when I gave the signal. Then I went round the cottage to the fateful window. My heart was pounding.

The captain called to the Cossack:

'Damn you! Having us on, are you? Or do you think we won't get you?'

Then he started banging at the door with all his might. Through the crack in the shutter I watched the movements of the Cossack, who was not expecting an attack from this quarter, then suddenly I tore off the shutter and threw myself head down through the window. There was a shot just by my ear and the bullet ripped an epaulette from my shoulder. The room filled with smoke and my adversary couldn't find the sword that lay beside him. I grabbed his arms, the Cossacks burst in, and within three minutes the criminal had been bound and taken away under escort. The crowd dispersed, and the officers congratulated me – as well they might!

How can one not be a fatalist after this? Yet who really knows if he believes a thing or not? How often our beliefs are mere illusions or mental aberrations.

I prefer to doubt everything. Such an attitude makes no difference to a man's determination – on the contrary, as far as I am concerned, I always go more boldly forward when I know nothing of what lies ahead. After all, the worst you can do is die, and you've got to die some time.

When I got back to the fort I told Maxim Maximych about all that I'd seen and experienced, and asked him what he thought about predestination. At first he didn't understand the word, but I explained it as best I could, whereupon he shook his head meaningly and said:

'Well, yes, of course . . . It's a tricky problem. As a matter of fact, those Asian triggers often don't work if they're not well oiled, or if you don't press hard enough. I don't go much on Circassian rifles either. Don't seem right for us somehow, and you're like as not to get your nose burnt with that short butt they've got. Their swords, though, now they really are something.'

He thought a bit, then added:

'Bad luck on that poor chap, though. He should have known better than talk to drunks after dark. Still, I suppose that's how he was meant to die . . .'

That's all I could get out of him – he's not at all keen on metaphysical discussions.

FATE ≠ LUCK?

NOTES

'Bela'

1. *valley of Koyshaur.* From Passanauer, where the main tributaries of the Aragva – the White Aragva and the Black Aragva – converge, the Georgian Military Highway follows the course of the White Aragva into higher mountainous terrain. Koyshaur (Kayshaur), a fort and staging-post, lay in this valley.

2. *Ossete driver*: The Ossetes were a tribe of the northern Caucasus, ethnically Iranian. They accepted Russian rule at the beginning of the nineteenth century and were docile in comparison with the mountain tribesmen who fiercely resisted Russian expansion. Ossetes were the regular providers of transport on the Military Highway.

3. *Aragva*: The River Aragva has a southward course from the main Caucasus range and joins the River Kura, which flows into the Caspian. The Military Highway from Tiflis follows its valley northwards.

4. *Kabarda pipe*: Kabarda is a region in the central Caucasus on the northern border of Georgia. Maxim Maximych's pipe was evidently a product of the local woodcraft.

5. *Stavropol*: Stavropol lies north of the mountainous area of the Caucasus. It was founded in 1777 and became the main administrative centre for the region.

6. *Alexei Petrovich's time*: General Alexei Petrovich Yermolov (1772–1861) was commander-in-chief of Georgia and the army in the Caucasus from 1817 to 1827. He conducted vigorous campaigns against the tribesmen in Chechnia, Daghestan and Kuban, built forts, and extended the area of Russian domination. He contributed also to the civil administration, improving the Military Highway and building mineral bathing

establishments. For old soldiers like Maxim Maximych – who refers to him familiarly by his forename and patronymic – he was a legendary figure.

7. *the Line*: See historical note at the end of the Introduction.

8. *Tatar . . . doesn't drink*: The Ossetes were mainly Christians (of a rudimentary kind); Tatars were Muslims for whom the use of alcohol was forbidden.

9. *Gud-Gora*: A mountain to the east of the Military Highway close to its highest point at the Krestovaya pass.

10. *Kabardians . . . Chechens*: The tribesmen of Kabarda and of Chechnia, which borders it on the east, were noted warriors and brigands.

11. *Kamenny Brod*: A fortified place (the name means 'Stony Ford') on the left flank of the Line in the flatlands of the Terek basin, south of the Terek on the River Aksai. Its fortification in 1825 was a sign of Russia's expansion southwards.

12. *Wish you good health*: The standard greeting of Russian soldiers to their officers.

13. *buza*: A kind of beer made from various grains.

14. *Terek*: One of the major rivers of the Caucasus. Rising in the mountains, it flows north to Vladikavkaz, then eastwards into the Caspian. The Military Highway, after passing over the Krestovaya, descends along its course to Vladikavkaz. In the 1830s it was effectively the border between the territory of established Russian domination and that still disputed by the native tribes. Maxim Maximych's 'fort over the Terek' is evidently the one already mentioned near Kamenny Brod.

15. *kunaks*: Among Caucasian tribes, a *kunak* is a friend with whom one has an obligation of mutual hospitality.

16. *Kuban*: The River Kuban flows westwards from the high Caucasus into the Black Sea near the Kerch Straits. It was a natural boundary between the southern limits of Russia and the untamed tribesmen south of the river, across which they made raids into the territory of established Russian rule.

17. *beshmet*: A tunic of middling length worn under a top-coat.

18. *Yakshi tkhe, chek yakshi*: 'A good horse, very good.'

19. *Cossacks*: Cossacks had their origin in the fifteenth century. They were a mixture of renegades, freebooters and fugitives from justice or economic exploitation, who formed independent settlements on Russia's southern and eastern fringes. Over time there was some interbreeding

with the local population. They were the frontiersmen, part farmers, part warriors, who were Russia's front line of defence and attack against her southern and eastern Turkic and Tatar neighbours. Cossacks were noted for their fine fighting qualities, as well as for their independent spirit – they played the leading part in the two great risings (of Stenka Razin and Emelyan Pugachev) which shook the stability of the Russian state in the seventeenth and eighteenth centuries. In the last quarter of the eighteenth century, after the Pugachev rising, the Cossacks were brought more firmly under control and became a potent arm of the Russian military, deployed both in war and in the maintenance of civil order. The various Cossack 'hosts' were named after the territory where they were settled – the Don, Kuban, Terek, Ural Cossacks, etc.

20. *Karagyoz*: The name of Kazbich's horse: it means 'Black Eye'.

21. *Yok*: 'No.'

22. *gurda*: Finely wrought blades made in the Caucasus and highly prized.

23. *yashmak*: The veil worn by Muslim women.

24. *Urus . . . yaman*: 'Bad Russian, bad!'

25. *Kizlyar*: A sizeable fortified town on the lower reaches of the Terek, some fifty miles from its mouth on the Caspian Sea; for anyone stationed at Kamenny Brod it would be the nearest outpost of civilization.

26. *Transcaucasian Tatars*: The native tribesmen (not necessarily ethnic Tatars) who occupied the territory south of the Caucasus range.

27. *the Krestovaya . . . learned Gamba calls it*: The Krestovaya mountain, at 8000 feet, is the highest point of the Military Highway. The pass of the same name runs 200–300 feet below its summit. The 'learned Gamba' is Jacques-François Gamba (1763–1833), a French traveller who made two extensive tours of southern Russia and the Caucasus in 1817–18 and 1820–4 with the object of promoting trade. He was subsequently the first French consul in Tiflis. He published an account of his travels – *Voyage dans la Russie méridionale, et particulièrement dans les provinces situées au-delà du Caucase* (Paris, 1826) – in which he describes travelling the Highway from north to south (Lermontov's narrator is doing the reverse). Evidently misled by the similarity of sound, he erroneously refers to Krestovaya (from Russian *krest*, 'cross' – referred to here) as 'Saint-Christophe'.

28. *Chertova Valley*: A slight depression that separates Gud-Gora from the Krestovaya.

29. *Saratov, Tambov*: Provinces (with provincial capitals of the same name) in south-east Russia. The reference to them as 'endearing' is ironic – a St Petersburger would consider them the ultimate in provincial backwaters.

30. *the Robber Solovey*: In a well-known *bylina* (folk epic tale) – *Ilya Muromets and Solovey the Robber* – Solovey ('Nightingale') is a formidable creature, whose prodigious whistle causes lakes to overflow, buildings to collapse, and men to fall dead.

31. *Peter the First*: Peter the Great (1672–1725), the modernizer of Russia, who fought many wars to extend and secure Russia's frontiers. His campaign against Persia in 1722 made him a pioneer of Russian expansion into the Caucasus region, though, as is noted, his expedition took him not over the main mountain range, but along the western coast of the Caspian Sea into Daghestan.

32. *Kobi*: The first staging-post on the northern descent from the Krestovaya pass.

33. *Baidara*: A tributary of the Terek.

34. *lezginka*: A lively dance of the Lezgians, the predominant tribe in southern Daghestan.

35. *Assembly Rooms in Moscow*: The 'Nobility Assembly' in Moscow was a social club for members of the gentry class.

36. *Shapsugs . . . Kazbich*: The Shapsugs were a warlike tribe of the western Caucasus (the Russian right flank). They fiercely resisted Russian encroachment and were subdued only in the 1860s. In the period of the novel there was, in fact, a noted warrior named Kazbich who fought against the Russians in this sector of the Line.

'Maxim Maximych'

1. *Terek . . . Vladikavkaz*: From the Krestovaya the Military Highway descends by way of the narrow valley of the Terek and the still narrower Daryal gorge, which lies between the staging-posts of Kazbek and Lars. Vladikavkaz, founded in 1784, was the principal town of the northern Caucasus. The name means 'Lord of the Caucasus'; in the Soviet period it was renamed Ordzhonokidze after the Georgian Bolshevik leader.

2. *the 'detachment' . . . from Yekaterinograd*: As is explained below, travel along the Military Highway was done in convoy with a military escort.

Yekaterinograd was the northern starting-point of the Highway and the convoy formed there. Pushkin in his *Journey to Arzrum* (1829) records that convoys departed twice a week, guarded by Cossacks, infantry and a single cannon. The convoy which Pushkin joined consisted of around 500 people.

3. *Kakhetian wine*: Kakhetia is a region of eastern Georgia, celebrated for its wine.

4. *Kazbek*: A prominent peak of 16,545 feet. It stands to the west of the Highway above the staging-post of the same name.

5. *Russian Figaro*: Figaro, the resourceful valet in Beaumarchais' plays *The Barber of Seville* (1775) and *The Marriage of Figaro* (1784), was noted for his independence and lack of respect for his 'betters'.

6. *samovar*: The Russian apparatus for making tea – an urn of water with an internal cylinder to convey the heat from the charcoal-burner at the base and a stand on the top holding a tea-pot. Strongly brewed tea is poured from the pot and diluted with hot water tapped from the urn.

7. *Balzac's thirty-year-old coquette*: The Marquise d'Aiglemont, heroine of the sketches that make up Balzac's *La Femme de trente ans*, first published in 1834 (augmented and revised in 1842). Lermontov's recollection of the work appears to be hazy: he attributes her lassitude to social over-exertion ('at the end of an exhausting ball'); in fact, she shuns society and her lassitudinous state results from the depression and disillusion brought on by an unsatisfactory marriage and doomed love-affairs. In making the comparison with Balzac's character, Lermontov may have had in mind the following:

There was something in the way she [sat] resting her two elbows on the arms of the chair and joining the finger-tips of each hand as if in play; the curve of her neck, the casual posture of her exhausted, though supple, body which seemed as if elegantly broken in the armchair, the limpness of her legs, the nonchalance of her bearing, the movements full of lassitude – all this revealed her as a woman without interest in life. . ., a woman who has long since despaired of the future and of herself . . .

Pechorin's Journal: Foreword

1. *Rousseau's 'Confessions'*: In his celebrated work, published post-humously in 1781–8, Jean-Jacques Rousseau (1712–78) was principally concerned with the revelation of his feelings and inner self rather than the events of his life which provide the frame of his work.

'Taman'

1. *Taman*: A small town on the Sea of Azov, near the Kerch Straits which link the Sea of Azov with the Black Sea. It is at the westernmost limits of the Caucasus region.

2. *Black Sea Cossack*: The Black Sea Cossacks at one time occupied territory on the northern shores of the Black Sea between the River Bug and the River Dniestr. In 1792 they were transferred to the eastern side of the Sea of Azov, between the River Kuban and Azov – though now not strictly on the Black Sea, they retained the name.

3. *Gelendzhik*: A Black Sea port some way down the coast east of the Kerch Straits.

4. *Crimean Tatar*: The thirteenth-century Tatar invasion established a Khanate in the Crimea. Though the Crimea was annexed to Russia in 1793, the population was still dominantly Tatar.

5. *There wasn't a single icon*: In an Orthodox household there would be at least one icon, in the principal room in the corner opposite the door. The absence of an icon is clear evidence of the 'unwholesomeness' of the place and its occupants.

6. *Then shall the dumb sing and the blind see*: Adapted from the prediction in Isaiah 35:6: 'Then shall the lame man leap as an hart and the tongue of the dumb sing.'

7. *Ukrainian ... Russian*: Ukrainian, the main language spoken in southern Russia (the Ukraine), is distinct from but closely akin to Russian. The blind boy, in addressing Pechorin in Ukrainian, clearly intends to confuse him as to his origins and create a barrier to too close interrogation.

8. *Phanagoria*: An ancient Greek port on the Sea of Azov close to Taman. In the eighteenth century the Russians built a fort there.

9. *undine*: By legend the undine was a water-sprite who married a mortal. The theme was developed in the romantic tale *Undine*, published in 1811, by the German writer Friedrich de la Motte Fouqué (1777–1843). A Russian reworking of Fouqué's tale in verse by V. A. Zhukovsky (1783–1852), the pioneer of Romanticism in Russia, was published in 1837.

10. *Young France*: Les Jeunes-France – an informal group of young Romantic writers in France in the 1830s. They looked to Victor Hugo as leader of the Romantic movement, and the remark here on breeding in women and horses stems from one of Hugo's poems, which refers to a young man who admired in Paris only 'well-bred women and race-horses'.

11. *Goethe's Mignon*: The ethereal and enigmatic girl of obscure Italian origin who is protected by the hero in Goethe's *Wilhelm Meisters Lehrjahre* (*Wilhelm Meister's Years of Apprenticeship*, 1795–6). Her resemblance to Lermontov's 'undine' is close – compare:

There was a strange quality in everything about the child . . . Going up or down stairs, she did not walk, but sprang; she would clamber up the baluster and in a trice be sitting aloft on a cupboard and then be still a while . . . Many days she said nothing, sometimes she gave answers to questions other than those asked, but always strange, and such that you never knew if she did it in jest or through unfamiliarity with the language. (Book 2, chapter 7)

'Princess Mary'

1. *Pyatigorsk . . . Mashuk*: Pyatigorsk is a spa town in the northern Caucasus noted for its sulphur springs. It stands above the River Podkumok (a tributary of the Kuma, which flows into the Caspian) on the slopes of Mount Mashuk. Pyatigorsk takes its name ('five mountains') from the nearby Mount Beshtau, which has five peaks. The town, founded in 1780, and its spa facilities underwent rapid development in the 1820s.

2. '*the last cloud of the dying storm*': The opening line of Pushkin's poem 'The Cloud' (1835).

3. *chain of snowy peaks . . . Kazbek . . . Elbrus*: The highest part of the Caucasus is the snow-covered ridge which stretches some 150 miles west from Kazbek (16,545 feet) to Elbrus (at over 18,000 feet, the highest mountain in Europe); between Kazbek and Elbrus there are several peaks of 14,000–16,000 feet.

4. *Elizabeth spring*: One of the principal mineral sources in Pyatigorsk.

5. *plain numbered buttons . . . of a line officer*: The distinction is drawn between the social élite who served in the guards regiments and the less privileged who served in the general army. The buttons of the former bore the imperial eagle, those of the latter simply the number of the division to which their regiment belonged.

6. *pavilion called 'The Harp of Aeolus'*: This round, columned structure is a fine viewpoint from which the whole Caucasus range is visible. It contains an Aeolian harp, a device with strings which sound when the wind passes through them (from Aeolus, ruler of the winds).

7. *cadet*: Grushnitsky was a *yunker* (from German *Junker*), in the Russian army a volunteer soldier of sub-officer status awaiting the opportunity of gaining a commission.

8. *St George's Cross*: The principal military decoration for valour in action. As a *yunker*, Grushnitsky held the 'soldier's Cross', the lowest grade of the order which was awarded to non-commissioned ranks.

9. *Mon cher . . . dégoutante*: 'My dear fellow, I hate men in order not to despise them, for otherwise life would be a too disgusting farce.' (The spelling *haïs* for *hais* is thus in the text.)

10. *Mon cher . . . trop ridicule*: 'My dear fellow, I despise women in order not to love them, for otherwise life would be a too ridiculous melodrama.'

11. *His name is Werner, though he's a Russian*: From the eighteenth century there was a large influx of Germans into Russia to take up service in the administration, army, and the professions. Werner evidently comes from one of these Russified German families. It is reliably claimed that Lermontov modelled Werner on Dr N. V. Maier, a military doctor who practised in the spa towns of the Caucasus and whom Lermontov first met in Pyatigorsk in 1837.

12. *Endymions*: In Greek mythology Endymion was a young man of ideal beauty.

13. *Cicero . . . the Roman augurs*: In his debunking treatise on divination Cicero quoted with approval the jibe of Cato who expressed astonishment that a soothsayer does not burst out laughing at the sight of another soothsayer (*De Divinatione*, II, xxiv).

14. *Your affair . . . stir*: The nature of Pechorin's 'affair' in St Petersburg, which had evidently led to his transfer to service in the Caucasus in an unprestigious line regiment, is not explained. He had most likely fought a duel.

15. *Chelakhov's shop*: The principal store in Pyatigorsk – it was still going strong in 1914, according to Baedeker's *Russia* of that year.

16. *with that private's greatcoat . . . a hero, a martyr*: On the assumption, that is, that Grushnitsky had been an officer and demoted for some interesting escapade.

17. *the grotto*: A grotto cut out of the rock on the slopes of Mashuk, a popular place of resort for visitors to the spa. (It is now named the Lermontov Grotto.)

18. *fièvre lente*: A slowly debilitating recurrent fever.

19. *the German colony*: The village of Karass (now Inozemtsevo, 'Foreigntown'), between Pyatigorsk and Zheleznovodsk, was settled in 1802 by missionaries of the Edinburgh Missionary Society and for a time was called Shotlandka (Scotchtown); with the arrival of German settlers in 1810 the small Scottish community dwindled and the village became known as 'the German colony'.

20. *en pique-nique*: 'On picnic excursions'.

21. *Beshtau, Zmeinaya, Zheleznaya, Lysaya*: Volcanic mountains in the proximity of Pyatigorsk, all between 2000 and 5000 feet.

22. *Mon dieu, un circassien*: 'My God, a Circassian!'

23. *Ne craignez rien . . . votre cavalier*: 'Have no fear, madam. I am not more dangerous than your cavalier.'

24. *Nogai's cart*: The Nogais are a Turkic people who occupy the steppe lands north of the Terek in the east of the Caucasus region.

25. *farthingales*: The farthingale was a hooped skirt distended on canes or whalebone. It went out of fashion in the eighteenth century.

26. *C'est impayable*: 'It is too ridiculous.'

27. *Charmant! Délicieux*: 'Charming! Exquisite!'

28. *the Chasm*: The Chasm (*Proval*), a popular excursion point in the neighbourhood of Pyatigorsk, is a deep cavern open at the top and with a sulphur spring at its base.

29. *Kislovodsk*. A spa town a few miles south-west of Pyatigorsk.

30. *one of the artfullest rogues . . . whose praises Pushkin once sang*: The reference is to P. P. Kaverin, a friend of Pushkin in the poet's youth, to whom he addressed several poems. He was noted for his wit and *bons mots* (the one quoted may not be of his best).

31. *bourgeois tragedies*: 'Everyday' tragedies involving 'ordinary' people. The genre developed from the late eighteenth century and represented a descent from the high tragedy of the classical period.

32. *Reader's Library*: A popular monthly journal, mainly literary, published in St Petersburg from 1834.

33. *titular councillors*: Lowly ranked officials in the civil administration: they came ninth (out of fourteen) in the Table of Ranks introduced by Peter the Great.

34. *Yermolov baths*: One of the bathing establishments in Pyatigorsk, named after General Yermolov (see 'Bela', note 6).

35. *her entire fortune – fifty serfs*: Before the emancipation of the peasants in 1861 the property of a Russian landowner was commonly expressed in the number of serfs he owned. An 'entire fortune' consisting of an estate with fifty serfs was not much.

36. *Narzan . . . heroes' spring*: One of the springs of Kislovodsk, celebrated for its carbonic water. 'Narzan' is derived from the native name, which means 'drink of the Narts' (a tribe of heroic warriors). It is still widely drunk in Russia.

37. *the air in Kislovodsk . . . Mashuk*: Kislovodsk is 1000 feet higher than Pyatigorsk ('the foot of Mashuk') and the air correspondingly more stimulating.

38. *Many are fond . . . never to do*: The lines are from Griboedov's comedy *Woe from Wit* (1823).

39. *Nero*: The tyrannical and self-glorifying Roman emperor who reigned AD 54–68.

40. *The intellect's cold observations . . . the heart*: The last two lines of the preface to Pushkin's 'novel in verse', *Eugene Onegin*, in which he describes the content of his work.

41. *Tasso's 'Jerusalem Delivered'*: Tasso's epic poem *Gerusalemme Liberata* (1575) is concerned with the siege and capture of Jerusalem by the crusaders in 1099. In Canto 13 the crusaders, needing timber to repair their siege-engines, enter a forest, but initially turn back when they find it possessed by demons and evil spirits.

42. *rock called The Ring*: Near Kislovodsk, a massive natural arch which forms a roughly circular gap in the limestone cliff.

43. *the Vampire*: The reference is to the 'hero' of the story *The Vampyre* published in 1819. It was the product of a ghost-story-writing exercise in Byron's circle in Geneva and was written by his friend and physician

John Polidori, possibly after a sketch by Byron himself. The principal character in the story is the sinister Lord Ruthven, who, before his death and return from the grave as a vampire, moves in society, wilfully destroying virtue and promoting vice wherever he can. The story enjoyed vogue status and was widely translated; a Russian version was published in 1828.

44. *your position*: The fact that Pechorin is under official disfavour, as evidenced by his posting, presumably from service in St Petersburg, to a line regiment in the Caucasus.

45. *son cœur et sa fortune*: His heart and his fortune.

46. *Apfelbaum*: A celebrated conjurer of the day who toured widely. He is known to have given performances in the spa towns of the Caucasus in the 1830s.

47. *Walter Scott's 'Old Mortality'*: Scott's novels were popular throughout Europe. A Russian translation of *Old Mortality* (1816) had appeared in 1824.

48. *remember Julius Caesar*: A reference to the various omens said to have preceded Caesar's last attendance at the Senate, where he was assassinated (44 BC).

49. *Finita la commedia*: 'The play [show] is over.'

50. *Yessentuki*: A Cossack village (later also a spa) about halfway between Kislovodsk and Pyatigorsk.

'The Fatalist'

1. *boston*: A card game involving the taking of tricks, akin to whist.

2. *faro or bank*: Card games in which the players lay stakes on cards to win against the holder of the bank.

3. *chikhir*: An unfermented Caucasian red wine.

PENGUIN MODERN CLASSICS

CALIGULA AND OTHER PLAYS
CALIGULA/ CROSS PURPOSE/ THE JUST/ THE POSSESSED

ALBERT CAMUS

'Few French writers of this century have been more versatile or more influential than Camus' *The Times*

Camus's four philosophical dramas illustrate the shift in his perception of the human condition. *Caligula* reveals some aspects of the existential notion of 'the absurd' by portraying an emperor so monstrous that in his search for freedom he destroys gods, men and himself. *Cross Purpose* portrays a universe in which cruel, inexplicable things happen to innocent and evil people alike. By the time of the overtly political plays, *The Just* and *The Possessed*, Camus dramatizes action and revolt in the name of liberty.

With an Introduction by John Cruikshank

WINNER OF THE NOBEL PRIZE FOR LITERATURE

PENGUIN MODERN CLASSICS

A HAPPY DEATH
ALBERT CAMUS

'Camus is one of those writers who … marks a reader's life indelibly' William
Boyd, *Daily Telegraph*

Is it possible to die a happy death? This is the central question of Camus's
astonishing early novel, published posthumously and greeted as a major literary
event. It tells the story of a young Algerian, Mersault, who defies society's rules
by committing a murder and escaping punishment, then experimenting with
different ways of life and then finally dying a happy man.

In many ways *A Happy Death* is a fascinating first sketch for *The Outsider*, but it
can also be seen as a candid self-portrait, drawing on Camus's memories of his
youth, travels and early relationships. It is infused with lyrical descriptions of the
sun-drenched Algiers of his childhood – the place where, eventually, Mersault is
able to find peace and die 'without hatred, without regret'.

Translated by Richard Howard

With an Afterward and Notes by Jean Sarocchi

WINNER OF THE NOBEL PRIZE FOR LITERATURE

PENGUIN MODERN CLASSICS

A CAPOTE READER
TRUMAN CAPOTE

'Vintage Capote ... There is a depth and clarity to his writing that captivates the reader' *Sunday Times*

Truman Capote began writing when he was eight and became one of America's most versatile and gifted authors. *A Capote Reader* contains much of his published work: his dazzling fiction, including *Breakfast at Tiffany's*, as well as his prolific output of short stories, travel sketches in which he evokes places from Tangiers to Brooklyn, portraits of his contemporaries such as Marlon Brando, Marilyn Monroe and Cecil Beaton, and his brilliant reportage and essays. His piece entitled 'The Muses are Heard', which recounts a trip to Communist Europe with the cast of *Porgy and Bess*, shows the chameleon-like talents of a literary legend.

'Demonstrates the unvaryingly high quality of Capote's writing and the exquisite, fairy-tale aspect of his talent' Edmund White

PENGUIN MODERN CLASSICS

THE FALL
ALBERT CAMUS

'Have you noticed that Amsterdam's concentric canals resemble the circles of hell? A middle-class hell, of course.'

Jean-Baptiste Clamence addresses a chance acquaintance in an Amsterdam bar. A successful Paris barrister – the epitome of good citizenship and decent behaviour – he has now come to recognise the deep-seated hypocrisy of his existence. His brilliant, epigrammatic and, above all, discomforting monologue gradually saps, then undermines, the reader's own complacency.

'Camus is the accused, his own prosecutor and advocate. *The Fall* might have been called "The Last Jugement"' Olivier Todd

WINNER OF THE NOBEL PRIZE FOR LITERATURE

THE STORY OF PENGUIN CLASSICS

Before 1946 ...'Classics' are mainly the domain of academics and students, without readable editions for everyone else. This all changes when a little-known classicist, E. V. Rieu, presents Penguin founder Allen Lane with the translation of Homer's *Odyssey* that he has been working on and reading to his wife Nelly in his spare time.

1946 *The Odyssey* becomes the first Penguin Classic published, and promptly sells three million copies. Suddenly, classic books are no longer for the privileged few.

1950s Rieu, now series editor, turns to professional writers for the best modern, readable translations, including Dorothy L. Sayers's *Inferno* and Robert Graves's *The Twelve Caesars*, which revives the salacious original.

1960s The Classics are given the distinctive black jackets that have remained a constant throughout the series's various looks. Rieu retires in 1964, hailing the Penguin Classics list as 'the greatest educative force of the 20th century'.

1970s A new generation of translators arrives to swell the Penguin Classics ranks, and the list grows to encompass more philosophy, religion, science, history and politics.

1980s The Penguin American Library joins the Classics stable, with titles such as *The Last of the Mohicans* safeguarded. Penguin Classics now offers the most comprehensive library of world literature available.

1990s The launch of Penguin Audiobooks brings the classics to a listening audience for the first time, and in 1999 the launch of the Penguin Classics website takes them online to a larger global readership than ever before.

The 21st Century Penguin Classics are rejacketed for the first time in nearly twenty years. This world famous series now consists of more than 1300 titles, making the widest range of the best books ever written available to millions – and constantly redefining the meaning of what makes a 'classic'.

The Odyssey continues ...

The best books ever written

PENGUIN (P) CLASSICS

SINCE 1946

Find out more at www.penguinclassics.com